Endangered

DELTA FAMILY ROMANCES #7

CAMI CHECKETTS

D1004410

Birch River
PUBLISHING

Copyright

Endangered: Delta Family Romances #7

Copyright © 2022 by Cami Checketts

All rights reserved.

Free Book

Receive a free copy of *Seeking Mr. Debonair: The Jane Austen Pact* at https://dl.bookfunnel.com/38lc5oht7r and signing up for Cami's newsletter.

Chapter One

Kylee Seamons scurried through the stadium gates of Veterans Memorial Stadium, checking over her shoulder to see if she'd shaken her tail.

The answer was a horrifying no, nyet, nein, non.

The lean man with a shaved head and eerie pale blue eyes stayed just close enough to keep her in his sights. She thought she'd lost him several times on the drive from Chicago to Boston, but he always turned up.

He caught her staring and turned away as if he were heading toward the Korean War Memorial.

Her stomach churned—and not because she'd subsisted on jerky, Snickers, and Red Bulls for the past sixteen hours. Had her shadow been sent by her grandmother, or did King Frederick's man know what she'd overheard? They'd been speaking in Polish and probably assumed if someone overheard them, they couldn't understand them. Polish wasn't Kylee's best language, but it was similar enough to Czech that she understood plenty.

Mimi, as her grandmother demanded Kylee call her, because she was "far too young and beautiful" to be called Grandmother, hadn't known Kylee was coming by that night. Kylee got cussed regularly for not stopping by. She had been praying for strength that night and felt prompted to go right at that moment. She'd hoped that meant Mimi would be gone or something. It wasn't easy to endure Mimi's berating. Her grandfather attempted to counteract the vicious diatribe, but even a pastor couldn't be that uplifting.

They were her only family, and it was twisted, but she felt she owed it to her deceased parents to keep trying to be there for her grandpa.

She hadn't meant to sign her own death warrant by visiting them last night.

With all the plastic surgery she'd endured over the years, Mimi certainly didn't look old enough to be the grandmother of a twenty-seven-year-old linguist and educator. She loathed the fact that Kylee had a figure curvier than Jennifer Lopez's and people often said she looked like a younger version of the famous actress. Mimi found something to fault about Kylee no matter what she tried. She had tried starving herself and every form of exercise known to womankind. Mostly, she tried to stay in the shadows.

Despite the frustration of hips and a bustline that would make Jessica Rabbit proud, Kylee kept up a diligent exercise routine of walking, Pilates, and dance. She ate healthy ... ninety percent of the time. She'd tried to stop eating ice cream for over a year, but that just made her as miserable as visiting Mimi. If she had any extra money, maybe she would hire a personal trainer and a dietitian. The inner-city school district in Chicago she worked at couldn't pay her any more, no matter how expensive living in the city was, and Kylee was diligent about saving. She refused to be reliant on anyone, most especially Mimi, and was prepared for every rainy day.

There was no one taking money at the gate of the classic stadium in Quincy, Massachusetts, just south of Boston. The lacrosse game had started an hour a half ago, and it had to be in the fourth quarter. Kylee was only grateful she'd made it and said a quick prayer in her head to thank the good Lord. When she'd thought of this plan as she escaped Chicago late last night, she hadn't known how it would work out, but Chandler Delta was the name that kept coming to her head as she prayed. She hoped it wasn't just her ten-year obsession with the incredible athlete that women the nation over would give up chocolate, or possibly even ice cream, for one date with.

Kylee had actually kissed the superstar, multiple times, back when they were sixteen. She wasn't sure that it counted as a relationship to him, but she'd spent the week in Colorado falling in love with Chandler. She'd never forgotten his confident appeal, the way he made her feel valued, or the connection and sparks she'd assumed they had between them. Mimi had seen them together and told Kylee that Chandler was out of her league and would forget her before they climbed on the plane to fly home. Regrettably, Mimi had been dead on. Chandler had easily written her off and forgotten her. He had never once texted or called.

Chandler had developed into an irresistible man—just ask all his dates—and a lacrosse superstar. Kylee was admittedly fascinated with him and just another crazy fan. She couldn't believe she was dropping her pride from being ghosted by him all those years ago and coming to him for protection for not just her, but the entire country. Apparently she had no pride, but Mimi could've told her that. It might be that she had no options, but she trusted in heaven above, especially as both her earthly and heavenly parents resided there. If they said go to Chandler Delta, she had to listen.

She heard a roar go up in the bleachers. At least the lacrosse game wasn't over yet. She didn't know what she would've done if she'd missed him. She had to find Chandler and pretend she was a rabid female fan. Well, that wasn't much of a stretch. She prayed he recognized her and wouldn't sic security on her before she had a chance to whisper her secrets. Then she could disappear with a clean conscience.

It had been too late to withdraw from her savings before she fled Chicago. She should probably hit an ATM since Creepy Eyes seemed to know where she was regardless. Luckily, she had over five grand in cash that she'd hidden in her apartment drawers. She'd used cash instead of credit cards for gas and food driving here so she wouldn't give Mimi a trail to follow. Turned out that had been a waste as Mimi's man, or whoever Creepy Eyes was, had stuck to her like glue.

Admiral Davidson "Papa" Delta, Chandler's grandfather, would've told her he and his family would protect her and sent someone for her. She knew he would. The problem was after she'd contacted Papa Delta five weeks ago, she'd suspected someone was watching her. So either they were tapping her phone or Papa's. This secret had to be shared in person.

She instinctively knew she could trust the Deltas, but she couldn't wait for Papa to extract her. Grandpa Seamons had shown up at her apartment late last night, two hours after she overheard the fateful conversation. He confided that someone was being assigned to eliminate her, and she needed to disappear. He wouldn't tell her who had assigned the hit. He'd offered protection, but she didn't know if she could trust even her own grandfather.

When she'd contacted Papa Delta, her grandfather's lifelong friend, the former-Admiral already had suspicions about her own admiral grandfather. But neither of them had known at that point it was her grandmother who was the evil linchpin. Kylee should've guessed, having known for years that her snarky grandmother was capable of dark deeds. Though Grandpa was a decisive and accomplished military leader, he was a controlled wimp in his own home. But was Grandpa in league with Mimi? She loved her grandfather and prayed he was innocent.

She shuddered at the fear and all the unanswered questions. Sick that she hadn't been able to shake Creepy Eyes and wondering when he'd try to "eliminate" her or if he was waiting to see what she did, and who she contacted, first. She'd driven the fourteen hours from Chicago to Boston, only stopping for food, drinks, the bathroom, and gas. She was exhausted and terrified after her personal *mauvais quart d'heure*.

Please help me get the info to Chandler. Then, if it be thy will, let me escape, she prayed.

She'd been so confused that she'd prayed last night and received the prompting to go to Mimi and Grandpa's at that moment, but now she believed it was for a higher purpose. She could prevent so many deaths by getting the information into the right hands. Her own life was inconsequential at this point. That thought made her gut wrench and cold fear prick on her skin, but she had to be brave and not think about being shot in the back at any moment.

Walking through a portal and into a lower section of bleachers, she took in the beautiful scene of a green turf field with thick trees surrounding the bleachers. It was the first of September and still green and warm on the east coast.

The fast-paced game of lacrosse captured her attention and for a moment, she watched the action as the Boston Cannons in their navy blue uniforms with red accents controlled the ball with quick passes, progressing closer and closer to the goal against some team in white and green uniforms.

Three passes were drilled so fast from one player to the next that her eyes were still catching up as number eighty-three, the talented Chandler Delta, fired at the goal. The white ball stung the back of the net, passing over the goalie's right shoulder so fast he reacted a fraction of a second too late.

The crowd went insane, and Kylee screamed along with them. She loved this game. She'd never been much into sports growing up, but on her one trip to Summit Valley, Colorado as a teenager, the irresistibly handsome and charming Chandler Delta had converted her into a lacrosse junkie. He'd taught her how to pass and catch with a lacrosse stick. He'd complimented her so sincerely and so often she almost believed him and shut out the snarky comments Mimi had whispered in her ear when her parents were alive and said loudly once they were gone. Chandler had taken her on precisely three "walks" into the forest where they'd shared some incredible kisses. She knew it had only been a fun fling for him as he'd promised to call and text, then never once tried to contact her after she went home with her parents and grandparents to Chicago. Her parents had been killed shortly after. That summer trip and the carefree, romantic, and fun time with Chandler lived in her mind as the best moments of her life.

She'd watched almost every college game he played at Syracuse and professional games with the Boston Cannons. He was amazing. Even if he had broken her heart as an impressionable sixteen-year-old.

"And Chandler Delta stings top shelf to make the score twelve to seven, with only two minutes left in the fourth."

As the crowd continued to scream, Kylee looked over her shoulder but didn't see Creepy Eyes. She eased along the bleachers and annoyed quite a few fans as she excused herself past clapping hands as they cheered and then past knees and feet as they settled back down to watch the next face-off. She pushed as far as she dared and finally created a spot for herself in the fourth row. She fastened her gaze on Chandler. Watching him play in real life was even more amazing than watching it on her computer.

The last two minutes of the game wound down far too quickly, and as the crowd counted down from ten, reality slammed back into her. She wasn't here to ogle the gorgeous superstar; she had to get him a very important message. Fingering the expensive jade and diamond necklace hidden under her blouse that her grandfather had given her, she worried Grandpa was as rotten as Mimi.

You're the rotten snitch, Mimi's voice said in her head.

Den mund halten, she commanded back. She could say shut up or be quiet in many, many languages.

Sadly, the voice never listened.

Kylee pushed that away and focused on Chandler. She had no clue how she would get to him, or how she would whisper secrets in his ear. She couldn't have Creepy Eyes turn his sights on Chandler.

The buzzer sounded, and the crowd exploded with cheers. Some people immediately headed for the exits. Quite a few others lingered, including Kylee. The rest of the fans were probably reluctant to relinquish the glorious feeling of a victory with their team, or maybe hoping the players would come talk to them.

Kylee prayed for some way to get Chandler's attention. Would he even remember her? She was an obsessed fan girl of his, but it had been years since they'd seen each other, and she'd put on twenty pounds.

Thirty, Mimi's snarky voice said in her head.

Càllate, she begged.

Keeping a positive self-image as a shapely girl in a thin-obsessed world was next to impossible, but she tried. Half-heartedly, but at least she hadn't thrown in the towel. Her mom and dad had believed she was the most beautiful, smart, hardworking, and charming person on the planet. When they were killed in an airplane accident, she'd had to endure the last two years of high school living with Mimi. Grandpa Seamons had loved her and tried to be there for her, but he was a stern military leader not a gushing parent, and nobody could overcome the snark and digs Mimi was capable of. How she missed her parents.

The Boston players started jogging around the stadium, slapping hands with the fans who surged down to the edge of the bleachers, hanging over the side for a chance to interact with their superstars.

Kylee's stomach hopped. This was exactly the opportunity she needed and had been praying for during the long hours of driving and hoping she was making the right move.

Looking around for Creepy Eyes, she still didn't see him. She climbed over the three rows in front of her and pushed her way between two teenage boys to somehow get Chandler's attention.

"Hey," one of the boys protested.

"Sorry," she said, giving him a desperate smile. "I have a huge crush on Chandler Delta."

He grinned back at her. He had her by half a foot, but that didn't mean much as she was only five-four because of her four-inch heels. As her grandmother would be happy to remind her, she was probably exaggerating her height just like she downplayed her weight.

"Lucky dude," the kid said. "You could have a huge crush on me."

She couldn't help but laugh. She was disheveled, her hair in a sloppy bun and her blouse and skirt wrinkled. She couldn't imagine she looked attractive right now. It was embarrassing, as she wished she could look her best for Chandler, but that wasn't the mission right now.

"Well thank you, sweet boy, but I think I'm about ten years older than you."

"You're so beautiful. I'm sure age wouldn't come between us." He winked, and she thought he was adorable. "Has anybody ever told you that you look like J. Lo?"

"*Oui.* I have heard that before." She was impressed he knew who J. Lo was. Wasn't Jennifer Lopez in her fifties? "I've always wanted a younger brother."

His nose wrinkled. "Gross. I don't want to be your brother. I want to take you out."

Players started surging past, and she had to ignore her crazy but complimentary teenage friend to make sure she didn't miss Chandler. Sometimes her high-school students hit on her, and it always made her laugh. Silly kids were just trying to get extra help or a better grade. She wasn't sure what this kid's excuse was, but she appreciated the bolster to her confidence as Chandler was approaching.

Her heart seemed to stop, then take off at a gallop. Her palms grew sweaty. She completely missed the hands of the two players before him, so focused on those incredible blue eyes, that irresistible grin, and his handsome face. His dark hair was mussed from his helmet and his jersey was drenched in sweat. She didn't mind. Maybe the fact that he wasn't clean and perfect would help him forgive that she wasn't.

She shook her head. It didn't matter. She had to discreetly get him alone, share the conversation she'd overheard, and then find a way to St. Lucia, the Caribbean island of her dreams, where Mimi and her hitman would hopefully never find her.

Chapter Two

Kylee could hardly catch a full breath as Chandler approached. He was right there. It was all she could do to not scream his name and beg him to help.

Chandler stopped a couple people away from her and cocked his head at a gorgeous, tall blonde. "Excuse me?" he asked kindly, like he sincerely wanted to hear what his fans were saying.

She leaned over the railing and begged him, "Can I have your jersey ... please?"

A couple other players streamed around him, laughing and obviously not wanting to wait.

"Chandler, always the ladies' man," a huge redhead, one of Chandler's teammates, said to a shorter, dark-haired guy.

"I'll give you my jersey," the dark-haired guy called to the blonde.

She ignored him, drooling over Chandler like every other woman in the stadium.

Kylee's stomach took a nosedive, along with all her romantic and never to be fulfilled dreams of Chandler being her someone special.

"Sure," he said, gifting the blonde with his charming grin.

He whipped off his jersey and handed it over. The blonde clutched the sweaty thing to her chest. Gross. Though Kylee would probably do the same if Chandler handed her his jersey.

Kylee's gaze was drawn to Chandler's chest, partially visible under the small chest pad, and his shoulders and abs that were clearly visible.

Oh, mon. Oh, my.

She, along with probably every other female in the stadium, let out a gasp at the sight of all that muscular gorgeousness. It wasn't fair for one man to be that appealing. Kylee had to remember she'd never be the type to date a perfect model athlete. From her social media stalking of his name, she'd seen Chandler on dates with so many beautiful women that it could make her sick enough to not want to eat ice cream that night. Luckily, she overcame that awful impulse.

She could use a generous serving of Rocky Road right about now.

"Do you want my shirt?" the blonde asked Chandler coyly.

Kylee's stomach turned over. Nope. She was too sick for even ice cream.

Chandler held up his hands and stepped back. "No thanks."

He moved on to the teenager right in front of her, slapping the kid's hand. His teammate flirted with the blonde about taking his jersey.

"Hey, man," Chandler said. "Thanks for coming."

"You're the best!" the kid called out.

"Do you play?" Chandler asked, and Kylee's heart softened to him again. How cute was he to give this kid some attention?

"Yeah, man. I'm a d-pole for Quincy High."

"Sweet. I'm going to make one of your games this spring. I love watching Quincy play."

"Do you mean it?" The boy's eyes lit up, and he leaned forward.

"For sure. You came to watch me I have to return the favor." Chandler was so confident and kind. Kylee had been half in love with him for years. If he kept this up, she'd fall the rest of the way and earn a "stalker chick" badge for her obsession. It was idiotic to love a confirmed ladies' man, but rational thought went out the window with him this close.

"Keep working hard," Chandler said.

"I will!"

Chandler moved to slap the next person's hand. Hers. It was surreal to have those blue eyes focus in on her. The world started spinning. She reached out her hand, needing to speak and quietly beg him to remember her and to meet her somewhere so they could talk in private. She couldn't make her mouth form words and feared he'd slap her hand and keep on moving.

He didn't slap her hand. Instead, he wrapped his hand around hers. His blue eyes lit up and his generous mouth curved in a happy smile. "Kylee Seamons." He said her name as if *she* were the superstar.

Kylee blinked at him. "You remember me?"

"Of course I remember you." He stared at her as if she were

13

the only person in his world. His gaze entranced her, and she almost threw herself over the railing and hoped he'd catch her.

You'd knock him flat.

Sessiz olun!

"What are you doing here?" he asked. "Do you still live in Chicago?"

She nodded dumbly, cleared her throat, and said, "I need you."

His eyes seemed to grow warmer, and his hand clasped hers tighter. "Oh, yeah?" he asked in a husky voice that made her hot from head to toe.

"Get in line, girlie," the blonde yelled from a few seats over.

Kylee's eyes widened in horror. It was one thing to be an obsessive fan girl, but quite another to let Chandler see that within moments of meeting him again. "Not like that," she tried to rush out.

"She told me she's had a crush on you for years," her teenage buddy piped in.

Oh, my!

Kylee tried to pull her hand free, mortification tracing through her.

Chandler was beaming, and despite her embarrassment, all of her hopes of him someday noticing her like he had when they were teenagers blossomed. Was the superstar really staring at her as if she was appealing and his next date? But she selfishly didn't want to be just some date to him. She wanted to be the one for him. Like he'd always been the one for her.

She shook her head to clear it. The grown-up Chandler Delta was a huge player both on the field and off, and she was too smart to let her heart get broken by the likes of him again.

Too late. You're drooling like he's a hot fudge sundae, that snarky voice said.

Faire taire, she hurled back.

"Chandler." She leaned closer. "We have to talk."

"All right." He cocked his head. "I'd love to."

His teammate behind him called out, "Come on, dude. Let me flirt with the brunette now."

"Nope." Chandler shot his teammate a death glare. "She's mine."

Kylee should've protested. She wasn't any man's property, but Chandler claiming she was his made her out of breath and faint.

"Hey, guys," Chandler said to her teenage buddies. "Help me out here?"

They both grinned. "Sure."

Chandler released her hand and Kylee felt the sting of disappointment. He'd been flirting with her just like he had the blonde and every other woman who flaunted themselves at him. She had to complete her mission, not let Chandler shuttle her off with the teenagers.

She started to tell him to wait, but he wasn't going anywhere. She was. The two young men next to her started manhandling her. Kylee cried out in surprise. The one boy took her legs and the other looped his hands under her armpits. They swept her off the ground and lifted her over the railing.

Kylee was about to tell them to stop before they dropped her, but strong hands reached up and she was lowered down and against the perfect, albeit sweaty chest of one Chandler Delta, aka superstar middie for the Boston Cannons and her lifelong crush. Time stopped as she stared into his blue eyes, so close, so appealing. She felt safe and happy and as if no time had passed since he'd held her close all those years ago.

"Thanks, guys," he told the boys.

"You're the best, Chandler!" one cried.

He tilted his chin to them as his arms were full of her.

Kylee heard a female voice, probably the blonde, saying, "Why would he choose *her*?"

Her neck tightened at those words. Why would he indeed? The connection from when they were teenagers? She'd believed their kisses were unreal and their bond unparalleled, but she'd dated a total of five different boys or men in her life, and none of them anywhere close to Chandler Delta's level of charm, so she didn't have a great comparison model. Could Chandler have felt the same about their short time together and never forgotten her? That was asking for an impossible dream. Possibly he felt a little nostalgia for home and the memories of those fun summer times.

Or more likely ... Papa Delta had told his grandchildren to watch out for her and Chandler was instinctive enough to notice she looked like she'd been driving since yesterday and was running for her life and had information to convey before she was murdered. So he'd gotten her into his arms to protect her and pretend it was a romantic interest. That made sense.

She hated to look away from him, but she searched the stadium quickly. Thankfully, she didn't see Creepy Eyes. But she could bet he was there, waiting her out. Would she endanger Chandler?

"I hate that I'm a sweaty mess the first time I get to hold you again in ten years." Chandler easily drew her attention back to him.

"You remember ... that?"

His blue gaze turned smoldering. "Beautiful Kylee ... I have never forgotten *that*."

Her entire body did a happy dance. She was lost in his blue eyes and the heady sensation of being held tight to his glorious body. She was in trouble. She was in a whole lot of trouble. She had no idea how to respond to his glorious proclamation, and her body was so hot she feared she'd combust.

Chandler turned and strode across the field and toward the locker rooms. Kylee wrapped her arms around his neck to hang on and was rewarded with one of his brilliant, irresistible smiles.

"I can't believe you came for me," he said. "Like a vision from heaven. Let me remedy the sweaty problem and then we can really get reacquainted."

Kylee had no clue if he was intoning what she thought he was intoning. Would he kiss her again? It was probably wrong to indulge in such deliciousness when she needed to get the message sent and be back to running for her life, but kissing Chandler as full-grown adults would be a memory she could take to the grave. Her superhero. Holding her in his arms. It was surreal.

She felt sadly that she had to set him straight about why she was here and get the information out as quickly as possible so she didn't spend too much time with him and put a target on his back. He was a Delta, her grandpa had told her each family member had years of training and an understanding of fighting, weapons, and subterfuge that was completely beyond her, but still... Creepy Eyes could shoot him in the back or something. She doubted her grandmother's flunky had any more idea of moral conduct than Mimi herself. Even worse if the man had been sent by King Frederick. The awful dictator was trying to take over Europe and blustering that if China or America tried to intervene, it would be nuclear winter for their countries. Well, she'd thought he was blustering until last night.

"Chandler," she whispered urgently.

"Yes, love?" He looked down at her with a beguiling smile as he strode across the field.

She tried valiantly to ignore the endearment. He was a flirt, and she would be smart not to lose her head. If only he wasn't her dream man and far too charming for anybody's good.

"You know about the situation with my grandpa and the Delta secret?"

His gaze got serious. He walked to an overhang that was sheltered from view of the fans and relatively quiet, but he kept on holding her in his arms as if she weighed nothing. Impressive strength these lacrosse players had.

"Yes," he said. "Do you have information for me?"

She nodded. "I overheard something terrifying. Now someone's following me, and my grandfather told me there's a price on my head."

"What? Kylee." He held her even closer. "Let's get you somewhere safe."

She shook her head. "I'll disappear after I give you the info."

He gave her a challenging look that made her even warmer than his flirtatious ones. "I am not letting you out of my sight if you're in danger."

"Chandler..."

"Don't," he warned. "I'll keep you safe. Where's your tail?"

She pushed out an exasperated breath. Her safety was not the most important thing at the moment, but she couldn't help but savor his protective nature. She answered his question. "I saw him as I was entering the stadium. He followed me from Chicago."

"Do you have a tracker on you?"

"I don't know." Her eyes widened. Could Mimi have put a tracker on her phone at some point, or dropped something in her purse when she wasn't looking? Her small purse was strapped across her chest. Should she ditch it?

"Okay. It'll all work out. Let's get inside. I'll hide you in the manager's office and we'll check your purse and phone for trackers before we sneak out of here." He gave her a smile that said he would enjoy the challenge of ditching her shadow. She only cared that he could accomplish such a deed. Was it wrong to let him protect her? To rely on him? Maybe, but she had no one else and no matter how she kidded herself, she'd probably end up dead if she tried it on her own. Then she'd never see St. Lucia—or have Chandler's blue eyes focus in on her again as he gave her that appealing grin. Even the Caribbean blue waters paled compared to Chandler's alluring gaze.

He started walking again as if it was all settled. She should've insisted she could stand on her own two feet, but with as shaky and exhausted as she was, Chandler carrying her was very, very nice.

Just like that, she was lying to herself again. Like when she claimed she was five-two or she hadn't gained weight recently or she only ate ice cream on special occasions. Was it really wrong to claim every day was a special occasion? Being in Chandler Delta's arms was definitely a special occasion, especially with his shirt off, even if he was sweaty and still had his chest protector on.

Chandler entered through a door. Suddenly, there was a cacophony of noise and the shocking sight of men in various stages of undress.

"Oh!" Kylee cried out, burying her face in Chandler's warm skin.

"Sorry," he mumbled. "It's the only way to the office where you'll be safe. I didn't dare go through the stadium and have your tail follow or intercept us. Guys!" he called. "I've got an innocent beauty here. Cover up."

The men started whooping and yelling at them. Kylee heard all kinds of offers, many of which made her think she was much more innocent than Chandler could understand if he hung out with these men daily. She didn't understand men at all, though, so maybe their language was normal for a men's locker room.

"*Muchachos locos*," she muttered.

"What was that?"

"Crazy boys," she translated.

"Annoying," he agreed.

He strode quickly with her in his arms and she did not lift her head. He smelled of salt and sweat and, amazingly, it didn't offend her.

A door banged open and then closed and Chandler lowered her feet to the ground but kept his arm around her. "You okay?"

"Yes, thank you." Her voice was too prim, and she needed to lift her gaze from his muscles. He was over six feet, so even with her heels on, she was eye level with his glorious chest.

She forced herself to raise her gaze and got lost in those blue eyes of his. She knew all the Deltas had those incredible eyes, but Chandler's had always seemed more intriguing to her than any of the other family members. They had the power to make her forget everything but him. Hypnotic eyes.

"You'll be safe here. Security won't let anyone into the locker room. I'll hurry and shower and then we'll de-bug you and make a plan." He gave her a winning smile, released her from his arms, and hurried out of the office, shutting the door behind him. Luckily, the window had drawn blinds over it so she couldn't see what might be happening out in that locker room.

She sat heavily in a hard chair and took slow breaths, hoping to calm her racing pulse as she fingered her jade necklace. Touching it usually calmed her, but not right now.

Chandler Delta. Holding her close. Claiming he would protect her. Her mind starting racing with visions of the two of them on the run, him sheltering her, being her hero, teasing and laughing together like they had that blissful week, stealing kisses any chance they got.

The office was suddenly sweltering hot. She fanned herself and made a firm promise. No ice cream tonight and no romance novel reading time. She didn't need to stoke the flame of romance in her mind.

She chuckled at herself and wondered if she was going insane. Tonight she might be dead or hidden away in a closet for her own protection. She might never eat ice cream or read a romance again.

But she might spend more time with Chandler Delta. She bit her lip. He was more appetizing than romance novels or ice cream. And that was saying a lot.

Chapter Three

Chandler rushed through his shower in a daze. His head pounded from all the emotion. The past few hours had been overwhelming, exciting, and worrisome. To go from the rush of a huge win in their last game of the regular season to Kylee Seamons appearing like a gift from heaven. Then to hear that she was in extreme danger, had information about her grandfather probably being a traitor, and needed Chandler's protection.

He'd happily protect her, even if she hadn't asked him to. If only he knew how to not get distracted by her beautiful face and curvy shape. He'd thought when he was sixteen and she'd visited his family in Colorado that she was the most beautiful, fun, and sweet girl in the world. He'd deluded himself into believing they had a connection that would last forever. When she told him goodbye at the end of her visit with her grandparents, she'd sweetly asked him to text her. He'd told her nobody could stop him from texting and soon he'd find a way to come visit her.

His first carefully composed text that night had gotten a heart-breaking write-off from her saying he'd just been a summer fling, that she had a boyfriend back in Chicago, and to please not bug her again. It had stung for a while, but he'd been young and eventually his heart had healed and he'd moved on.

Or so he'd talked himself into believing. One interaction with the grown-up Kylee and he was right back to his teenage self, plotting and hoping he could spend the rest of eternity with her.

Comments floated around him, most of them directed at him or trying to bait him. He loved his teammates, but some of them were crude idiots.

"Delta, what's with you and the gorgeous brunette?"

"Where do I get me a hottie like that?"

"Delta gets all the women."

"Seriously. They're all impressed with his huge sponsorships."

"She has the *sweetest* body I've seen in years."

"She's way too hot for the boy scout. He wouldn't even know what to do with a woman that fine."

Chandler ignored all of them, rushing to his locker and quickly loading up his gear bag. They loved to tease that he was a boy scout because he didn't sleep around or a crazy Christian because he prayed before and after each game.

Speaking of which—he'd never needed communication with heaven so much.

He sat on the bench by his locker in semi-privacy, clasped his hands in front of himself, and thanked the good Lord for a successful, safe game and for sending Kylee to him, then he begged Him to know how he could help Kylee, keep her safe, and do what was best for the Detail Protection Detail and his family back home in Colorado protecting it.

Straightening, he was grateful most of the men were still in the open area or by the showers, bantering and enjoying chattering after the game.

Ty came around the corner. His dark eyes glinted. "Wow. Beautiful brunettes just falling into your arms now?"

Chandler smiled at his friend. "I'm just that good."

Ty chortled at the line some opposing player had taunted them with back in college, when the truth was the guy's stick was illegal and he'd been a cheap shot as well.

"Hey, I've got to take off for a few days," Chandler said.

"With the beautiful brunette?"

He nodded. "She needs help with some family trouble. It's an emergency."

"I'd give her some ... trouble. You don't see a face or body like that every day."

"Over my physically incapacitated body," Chandler snarled back at him. He was right. Kylee was unique and gorgeous. Her appealing dark eyes, full lips, and insanely generous curves made him think he'd better add to his prayer a plea to keep his thoughts and intentions pure. Just the feel of her in his arms had been irresistible. And he'd held a lot of women in his arms. The media, and the woman who begged him for photos with them, tried to make him out as a womanizer. He dated a lot, but he rarely kissed his dates, and he never went past kissing.

"That can be arranged, too." Ty grinned, then laughed. "Good crap, buddy, I'm just trying to rile you. I'll stay away from her."

He pushed a hand at his short, dark curls. "Wouldn't want her to dump your butt for me and break your heart."

Chandler was ready to throw down right here and now, but Ty interrupted him by asking, "You want me to smooth it over with Coach?"

He nodded. Ty was the team captain and the players' liaison. The coaches were actually meeting with some league officials about the playoffs, or they'd be in the locker room right now. They'd asked the team to shower and plan on a team meeting after the head coach's hoorah speech. They wouldn't like Chandler skipping out on the celebration or the plan for playoffs and practices leading up to the first round.

"I'll call him when I know the details," he said. "Hopefully I don't get benched for the playoffs, but this is important."

"She looked important," Ty teased. "But seriously. You're Chandler Delta. I don't think there's a coach on the planet idealistic enough to bench you during playoffs for missing a meeting and a few practices."

"You never know." Chandler admired coaches who stuck by the rules they laid out, but he'd seen a lot who bent those rules for the superstars. He'd tried to never take advantage of the fact that he was one of the stars. He was always on time, ate clean and didn't drink so he could perform well, and worked harder than anyone on the field. He thought those facts might help convince the coach he wouldn't be skipping if this hadn't been a real emergency. "Thanks, man."

"Anytime."

"Oh, also, can I trade you cars?"

Ty's brow squiggled. "What? Why?"

Chandler had no idea how to explain and hoped he wouldn't put his buddy in danger, but it was more of a precautionary measure. If the guy tailing Kylee was savvy enough to find out who number eighty-three was, the player that had carried Kylee off the field, and then it was a quick search through an easily accessible vehicle registration office and he'd have Chandler's vehicle and license plate. He didn't think the guy would hurt Ty once he saw he wasn't the right person and Kylee wasn't with him.

He shrugged, unable to explain.

"You in trouble, man?" Ty stepped closer.

Chandler lowered his voice. "Kylee might be." That was as much as he could give him.

"All right, then." Ty pulled out the keys to his Porsche and handed them over.

"You're a good friend," Chandler said, meaning it deeply.

"Tell me about it. I don't let just anyone take my baby."

Chandler chuckled and handed over the keys to his Chevy truck. The guys liked to tease him that his four-door truck didn't fit in the city and hampered his "chick magnet" image, but he didn't care. He wasn't a cowboy like his older brothers Thor and Greer, but he subscribed to their theory that a real man drove a truck and always had a knife in his pocket. The only time he didn't carry a knife was on the field and at the airport.

"Thanks again."

He slapped his buddy on the shoulder, slung his large lacrosse bag over his shoulder, and hurried toward the office he'd stowed Kylee in. Anticipation to see her again thrummed through his veins. She'd looked incredible in a fitted button-down shirt and pencil skirt. Not many women could boast curves like hers. Most of the women he knew starved themselves into a tragically thin state, and he was often afraid he'd break them if he pulled them close. He loved Kylee's dark brown, long-lashed eyes and smooth, beautiful face. Some men liked women all made up, but not Chandler. He'd take the fresh-faced innocence of Kylee any day over someone like that fake-looking blonde who'd asked for his jersey.

Pushing the door open, he stared in awe as Kylee was folded in half in some unnatural yoga position. He had no clue how she did that in her fitted skirt, and he thought she was the most appealing woman he'd ever encountered.

"Hey," she managed, straightening, tugging at her shirt and looking adorably embarrassed, her cheeks turning pink.

"Don't stop on my account. That looked ... uncomfortable." That was not what he wanted to say. Where was the famed Chandler Delta charm when he needed it?

She smiled at him. "I've been sitting in a car for over fourteen hours. Everything is stiff." He shut the door behind him and eased in closer. Her gaze traveled over him and she said in a rush, "You clean up nice. Though you also looked incredible with no shirt on."

His brows rose, and he felt very, very happy. "Thank you." He wanted to engage in an invigorating flirting discussion, but he had to put her safety first. "Do you want to tell me what's going on?"

She glanced around nervously. "Can we go somewhere safe to talk?"

"For sure." He pridefully wished he could take her to his restored Colonial home near Wollaston Beach. But if he was worried about driving his own vehicle, he definitely didn't think they should go to his house and let whoever was stalking her walk right in. "But first, can I look through your purse and phone to make sure they aren't tracking you?"

She nodded and handed over her purse. She said nothing as Chandler pulled everything out and put it on the desk. There wasn't much—a floral wallet with cash, credit cards, a Cold Stone gift card, and her driver's license, coconut-scented lotion, a packet of tissue, her phone, keys, mint lip gloss, a bottle of Advil, a few ... women's things, a paperback romance novel with a couple entwined in each other's arms on the cover, and a dark chocolate almond bar.

He couldn't help but smile. "What are you reading?"

She gave him an impertinent smile. "*Her Crazy Rich Fake Fiancé* by Jennifer Youngblood. It's fabulous. You should read it."

"Maybe I will." He grinned, but then he made himself focus, going over the items quickly but finding nothing. He turned the purse inside out and inside a small pocket, he found a round tracking device about the size of a nickel. He held it up.

Her eyes widened. "She was tracking me."

"She? I thought it was Admiral Seamons." But something was niggling at his brain. He was distanced from the protection of the Delta Family secret because he didn't live in the valley, but he'd gone home for Thor and Shelly's wedding last month and gotten a thorough update from Papa. Nelson Palmer, the man who'd sent three mercenaries to steal the secret and then tried to force Greer's girlfriend, Emery, to go after it, had said something about whoever sent him being a "her."

Kylee glanced around as if the ears had walls. Actually, this device could be a listening device.

"Let's chat soon," he said, standing and hurrying to put every-thing back in the purse except her phone, which he put in a desk drawer. Her brow squiggled at that, but she had to know how easily she could be followed through her phone. He pocketed the tracker.

"You're keeping it?" she whispered.

"For a minute." He tried to smile reassuringly as he took her hand and led her from the office.

She got a few hoots and offers from nearby players. Chandler was ready to show them exactly how in-depth his training and fighting abilities were. He might not be as advanced in military skills as most of his family, but he could easily dismantle any of these guys. He tightened his grip on her hand, waved the idiots off in what he hoped looked like an easy-going manner, and hurried her toward the players' parking lot.

He glanced around and asked her, "Do you see him?"

He saw what looked to be fans waiting for players to come out, but nobody that raised any flags.

She looked around nervously. "No."

"Okay. Let's go." He walked behind some vehicles and then saw what he was hoping for. A food service truck loading up the unused fresh food from their concessions stand. He ushered Kylee in that direction and, luckily, the crew headed back inside for another load without locking the truck. Chandler opened the back door and slid the tracker under a tray of bread.

"Smart." Kylee smiled brilliantly at him.

He grinned back, hoping he could get her somewhere safe and then they could get reacquainted like he'd told her earlier. Shutting the door, he took her hand again and led her to Ty's red Porsche 718.

"Not the most subtle car," she said.

He grimaced as he got her door and darted a gaze around. She was right. He should've traded Carson for his white Maxima, but he wasn't sure he trusted Carson with his truck. They'd drive the Porsche to a rental car company and get something different. Ty would kill him later for leaving his baby, but the rental company wouldn't damage it.

"We'll trade it out soon," he promised, ushering her into the seat.

Hurrying into the driver's seat again, he glanced around but only saw a few fans who called and waved when he looked their direction. He waved back but hurried into the car, dropped the keys in the console, and slid on some of Ty's sunglasses.

He drove out of the parking lot, not even sure which direction to go. Maybe it didn't matter until he had her story, passed the info on to Papa, and they made a plan to keep her safe, but he found himself turning north toward Boston and, more specifically, the airport. They'd have the largest rental car companies.

"Chandler." Kylee's hand on his arm distracted him. "That's him." She pointed at a tall, bald man staring at them from over the heads of a young family on the street corner. The guy had eerie pale blue eyes.

Chandler wanted to pull over and take care of the guy right now, but the man slid a 9mm out.

"*Zut allors!*" Kylee screamed.

Chandler thought that was French, but he had no idea.

The guy started taking shots at the Porsche from over the

family's heads.

People screamed and hit the ground. Bullets dinged off the car.

Ty was going to fillet him.

"Get down," Chandler begged Kylee. He gunned it away from the man, not sure if he was trying to take out their tires or kill them.

Kylee bent over and prayed audibly. Chandler hated that she felt threatened. With no weapons on him but his knife, and not being willing to risk Kylee or an innocent bystander being shot, he could only use the Porsche's power to get away.

He saw the shooter in his rearview, pocketing the gun and scrambling the other direction, probably realizing he had to get his vehicle.

Crap. Hiding the tracker and trading vehicles would not be effective now. Especially swapping vehicles with Ty. The Porsche was a pretty and too-visible target. The only good news was that the Porsche did zero to sixty in four-point-eight seconds and could go over a hundred and sixty miles per hour.

Chandler's hands were sweaty as he gripped the steering wheel. He looked over at Kylee. "He ran for his car. You can sit up."

She did, but she was visibly trembling.

Chandler wrapped his hand around hers and squeezed. "We'll be okay. I'll keep you safe."

"Thank you." Her dark eyes were fixed on him as if he were her hero.

Chandler said a desperate prayer that he could keep her safe. The thought of something happening to Kylee made his own hands tremble.

Chapter Four

Luckily the 3A was really close to the stadium, so Chandler wasted no time getting on the freeway and weaving around slower traffic.

"Tell me what you overheard," he requested. A man taking shots out in the open like that meant whoever was after her didn't care about secrecy and wanted her silenced quick.

Kylee wrung her hands together and kept looking over her shoulder. "I know your Papa thinks my Grandpa Seamons has leaked info about some secret your family protects."

He nodded. The fewer people who knew about the secret, the better, but they'd all been stumped when over the past four months five different Navy men associated with Admiral Seamons had known about or come after the secret. Papa and Admiral Seamons had served together and were lifelong friends. Papa didn't want to think one of the select people who had knowledge of the secret outside the Delta family would betray him, but everything linked back to Seamons. And then Kylee had called Papa less than two months ago to say she thought her grandfather was scheduling a meeting with the depraved dictator King Frederick's right-hand man, General Carl Phillip. General Phillip had been killed a few weeks ago by Chandler's impressive Navy SEAL brother, Aiden. It seemed everything was escalating regarding the secret and Frederick's demented plans of world takeover.

Chandler might not make the playoffs if Kylee's information was critical enough to warrant a hit man following her. That should be the last thing on his mind, but he'd dedicated most of his life to lacrosse.

He focused on the road as he slid around a mini-van, then glanced back at her.

"I don't think it's my grandpa. At least I hope he's not involved. It's all Mimi." She shuddered as she said the name.

His brows lifted. He could remember Kylee's high-strung and very fake-beautiful grandmother from their one summer visit. She'd been cordial to all of them, but his siblings and cousins had all expressed that Admiral Seamons "trophy" wife was not very pleasant to be around if another adult wasn't within earshot. She'd said snarky comments to everyone, mostly Chandler because of his obvious interest in Kylee.

"Nelson Palmer mentioned a 'her' as if a woman was his boss and contact, not the Admiral," Chandler mused.

"Really?"

He sped around a Lexus F Sport. Luckily no cops ready to slow him down yet, and he didn't see the man from the street corner, but the guy might be smart enough to stay back and shadow them until he thought he could take them out. The Porsche wouldn't be hard to tail.

He nodded. "That adds up. So what did you overhear and when?"

"Last night, I dropped by my grandparents' house to say hello. They were hosting a large party, which they often do. Mimi loves to host."

He nodded for her to continue.

"The security let me park in the back and I came in through the kitchen entrance. I heard voices coming my way, and one of them was Mimi's. So I hid in the pantry."

Chandler's gaze darted her way again, and he almost rear-ended a Tacoma. "You knew something was off that quick?" He slowed his speed and waited for a gap to get around the small truck.

"No. It's just instinct to avoid Mimi. I hoped to find Grandpa first and have him and a crowd insulate me from her. That's the only way I get through the obligatory visits."

"I remember when you came to visit you didn't have a great relationship with her, but she vocally told my mom it was just 'teenage issues' and would get better."

"It's gotten worse. Especially once my parents passed, and I had no one who ..." She waved a hand and he wished she'd kept going. "Anyway. I don't know who the man talking with Mimi was, but he said something about King Frederick himself coming to meet with her."

Chandler about wrecked the car. Ty would skin him. Wrecking would be worse than the bullet holes already in it and ditching it at a rental car company.

"What? How? Why?" he demanded, rapid firing questions she

probably had no answers to. Most of his hopes and dreams of reconnecting with Kylee were pushed to the side.

"I have no idea, but they said something about a private jet registered in a man's name who had no terrorist or criminal activity. Think about it. It wouldn't be that hard to sneak into America on a private plane. I've flown into private airports. No security and the pilot checks your passport."

"I guess you're right. I should call Papa and let him know. Do you have a time frame?"

"No, but there's more."

His palms were sweating against the steering wheel. He checked the rearview again, not seeing anything suspicious. He'd been trained throughout his youth on how to fight with his hands and with a variety of weapons. He'd been trained in hostage and kidnapping situations, first aid, tracking, and high-speed chases. He was a Delta and instinctively he should've been all over this dangerous situation, but the fact was he'd spent his free time throughout high school, college and since playing lacrosse. His lacrosse career was his passion and his talent. He wished Aiden was here.

"Okay," he prompted her.

"So I hope I'm wrong about this, but basically the guy promised that because of her support and inside information, he would give Mimi two days' lead time before Frederick decimates the U.S. with his arsenal of nuclear weapons."

Chandler's stomach turned over. There were a lot of rumors that Frederick had nuclear weapons, but to his knowledge, nobody had confirmed or denied it. "You think he'd dare? You think he even has them?"

"I do." She nodded. "The guy claimed he's been procuring and even building nukes for years, and after he gets his hands on the Delta weapon, it's lights out for America."

Chandler knew there was no way to defend from an all-out nuclear attack. The U.S. hoped their huge arsenal of weapons would keep them safe from an enemy daring to fire. It was simply a deterrent. "But we'd fire on them from our bases throughout the world," he pointed out.

"They're planning on that. The weapons that the U.S. bases get off before they're destroyed, and the nukes that are based outside the continental U.S., will target Frederick's known locations in Banida, Germany, and Poland, but Frederick, his leaders, and a good portion of his army will be far away when that happens. He doesn't care about the men he has to leave behind, the innocent people he kills, or the long-term effects of radiation."

"That's even more terrifying."

"It is," she agreed.

All the visions of simply passing on some tip she had to Papa and then getting the dream woman of his teenage years alone, having her tell him she was wrong for writing him off and him forgiving her, and then effortlessly picking up the incredible relationship they'd been developing ten years ago evaporated. This was much more serious than he'd envisioned. This was the end of the world, World War III, with everyone and everything he knew and loved blasted off the planet kind of serious.

Sheesh. Chandler just liked to run fast, dodge, push, use impressive foot work and stick-handling skills so he could shoot a small ball at a goal. He didn't want to face this. At the same time, he'd known since he was a child that something like this could come his way. He'd been prepared for everything, including world-ending catastrophes.

Now to remember that training, keep Kylee safe, and help save the world.

"And he also thinks whatever the Delta family weapon is will not only protect him but make him the most powerful man on earth. Even more powerful than taking out America. He thinks China, North Korea, Russia, and any other countries with nuclear weapons or any kind of military force will bow to him when he has the Delta weapon."

Chandler saw the exit for the Boston-Logan Airport ahead. He buzzed over to the right lane, only earning one angry honk.

"Is he right?" she asked.

He sped off the exit and had to admit, "I have no idea. I don't even know if it's a weapon."

"What? *Porcaria!* I thought the Deltas at least knew what it was."

He shook his head, feeling a little inept and a lot helpless. "Only Papa and whoever the Secret Keeper is." Chandler had always been grateful that he wasn't the Secret Keeper, as he couldn't have pursued his passion for lacrosse. That was a level of responsibility he thought Colton, Esther, or maybe Aiden should take on, but so far nobody had claimed that knowledge.

"Dang. It would help a lot if we knew what the weapon was capable of. The only good news is if your family can keep him from the Delta weapon, he won't kill hundreds of millions of Americans."

This was insane, and horrifying. Chandler mulled over what to do as he followed the signs for rental cars. He didn't know if he should tell her, but the truth was he wasn't even certain it was a weapon. It could be the holy grail, the arc of the covenant, or a cure for chemical warfare for all he knew. Papa had never said the word "weapon" in regard to the secret. Only outsiders had called it that.

"Are we getting on a plane?"

"I don't think so yet. Your grandparents could easily track us then, as we'd have to use your I.D. for a commercial flight. Let's change cars, get Papa's advice, and then go find somewhere to stay tonight. You're probably exhausted."

"I am," she admitted.

"Why didn't you just contact Papa Delta again after you over-heard the info?"

She bit at a fingernail and looked so appealing he got distracted. They ran into a slow-moving line of vehicles trying to get into the rental car return. He didn't appreciate the delay, but he was able to stop the car and look at her. He appreciated that opportunity.

"When I called him," she said, "less than two months ago, I started feeling like someone was tailing me and Mimi got meaner with me than ever. I'm pretty sure she has my phone tapped."

"One of the reasons I left it behind," he said. "That was smart of you not to call again." She might not have made it to him if her grandma realized the information she had overheard.

"Thank you." Her voice quavered.

Chandler crept forward in line. "Let's change cars and then we'll call Papa as soon as we get some distance from 'Creepy Eyes." He smiled at her, and she returned it.

"I should come up with a better name, but ..."

"It's a great name for a loser who would stalk a beautiful woman."

Her eyes widened. "I'm not ..." She looked away from him.

Chandler studied her gorgeous face, wanting her to accept the compliment. Was it possible she didn't know how perfectly irresistible she was?

A loud horn blared from directly behind him. He looked up and there was a huge gap in front of him, but it was by no means the end of their destination. Him moving forward would not get the guy through the line any quicker.

He edged forward until he was up to the next vehicle's bumper.

Looking back at Kylee, he wanted to compliment her again, find out if she was dating anyone, talk about what she'd been up to the past ten years, ask how her job was going, but he needed to stay focused with the magnitude of the threat hanging over not just the Deltas but their entire nation.

"Did they find you in the pantry?" he asked to finish out her story.

"No. I stayed until I was certain they were gone, and then I snuck out and drove home. Too upset and confused to think straight, honestly."

"I can imagine. How'd you know you were in danger?"

"My grandpa came by late that night. He told me the security guards ratted me out and then Mimi found me sneaking into the pantry on the security cameras. She claimed I was spying on them. He didn't give me much, so I lied and said I hadn't heard anything or been trying to spy. That I'd just been hiding because I wanted a treat and didn't want Mimi to catch me." She gave him a sad smile. "Mimi hates it when I eat."

"When you eat?" That was the weirdest thing Chandler had ever heard. His granny was in heaven now, but it had seemed to bring her great joy to feed all of them and have her grandchildren thank her and rave that she was the best cook in the world.

Her voice dropped and sounded scratchy. "He said he didn't believe me, which made me feel bad even though I was lying, and asked me to confide in him what I'd heard. I just kept claiming I hadn't heard anything. He finally gave up but told me I needed to get away and offered protection. I didn't know if I dared take it, but I told him I'd think about it. I asked him why I needed protection and he said," she cleared her throat and then squeaked out, "Mimi was sending someone after me and she would kill me if I told anyone what I'd overheard."

His stomach clenched.

"I lied again and said I hadn't heard anything. His eyes said he didn't believe me and he asked me to please confide in him, but he finally gave up. He told me to call him if I saw anything out of line or was ready to share with him. He promised he'd come or send his men if I was in danger. As soon as he walked out the door, I packed and took off pretty quick."

Another horn honk and Chandler startled. He was tempted to wave at the guy with only one of his fingers. He pulled forward instead. He didn't need to deal with some angry driver right now.

"Your own grandmother would try to kill you?" he asked, doubt creeping in even though he didn't want her to hear that. Yet if her grandmother had been colluding with King Frederick, she was pretty evil, maybe low enough to even kill her own blood.

"Nobody has any idea what she's like," she said stiffly.

"Do you think your grandfather is involved? He acted like he didn't know what she'd said?"

"Yeah." She shook her head. "I have no idea if he's involved. He's always tried to protect me and seemed like the most loyal patriot, but I don't know what he's endured from Mimi. Maybe she's broken him or he's put on blinders because he doesn't want to know she's evil. She runs him at home, that's for sure."

He pondered her words. Papa Delta was going to have a mess on his hands. Luckily, Papa was smarter and had better connections than anyone he knew. But what if those in authority who could stop Frederick wouldn't believe what Kylee had overheard? America wasn't involved in the conflict and many wanted to keep it that way. Papa would also have to keep the Delta secret out of anything he shared with government or military officials. What if Frederick somehow got through their defenses and actually stole the secret? Even now, he could be sending more mercenaries after it. Was he at the root of all the recent attempts?

His mind was whirling. He wanted to call his grandpa right now. Should he wait until they changed cars? He worried this couldn't wait.

He was creeping forward in line when he caught a glimpse of movement out of his side window, a man moving fast toward his door.

He turned and looked just as Kylee gasped, "Creepy Eyes. *Oh mierda!*"

Chandler saw the man with eyes so pale they almost looked colorless raising a gun just outside his window. He didn't stop to think as he clicked unlock, lifted the door handle, and then slammed the door into the man as hard as he could. The guy was flung backward and hit the pavement on his back.

Shoving the car into park, Chandler told Kylee, "Get out quick."

He pushed out of his door and assessed. The man was stirring. The hit hadn't knocked him out. He stomped on the hand holding the gun and the man grunted in pain, then Chandler stripped the 9mm, hit the butt of the gun into the man's forehead, and shoved the pistol into the back of his waistband. He hated to take this filth's weapon, but he desperately needed it. If he'd been able to go home, he'd be armed to the teeth, but as it was, all he had was his knife and this pistol, and this situation was escalating out of control.

The man was out cold, but people were honking and yelling, some getting out of their cars to gawk.

Kylee made it around to the driver's side, staring down at the man in horror. Chandler reached back in, grabbed his phone and pocketed it, and fished out a Cannons' hat from his lacrosse bag. He shoved it on. Luckily, he had sunglasses on from driving. Leaving his gear bag that wouldn't do much more than slow him down, he sheltered Kylee with his arm and ushered her away from the scene.

People started yelling louder, especially the jerk from behind him, who'd jumped out of his car and looked ready to fight.

Chandler looked back and pointed. "This man just tried to kill us, and he's got friends coming to finish the job. I'd suggest you get back in your car and call 911."

The guy's mouth flopped open. He scrambled back into his car and slammed the door.

Chandler walked quickly away and into the car rental terminal with Kylee pressed close against him, hoping nobody was taking pictures to show to the cops or the news if they showed up, but they probably were. Ty's car and Chandler's gear bag would trace Chandler to the scene. He hoped the hit man had a rap sheet and the police would know Chandler wasn't the bad guy, but it was never great to flee a scene. He also wished he would've questioned Creepy Eyes before knocking him out cold. Aiden would've gotten the truth out of the guy and somehow secured the scene as he rescued the girl and got a long kiss. Chandler was only grateful they hadn't been shot.

The farther they got into the covered parking garage, the fewer people were gaping or saying stuff to them. He hurried to the far end where cars were lined up, all ready to go. He reached a silver Toyota Camry that was close to an exit and had the keys in it. Looking around, he was relieved there wasn't an employee close.

Kylee glanced up at him. "What are we going to do?" she asked. Her dark eyes were anxious, but she was impressively not flipping out.

Chandler stared into her deep-brown eyes and for a brief second, all the questions didn't matter. He would do anything to protect her and to have her look at him with trust and appreciation in those beautiful eyes. If only he was better at the military op stuff. He should've brought his lacrosse stick. He could take somebody down with that easily.

He smiled as he ushered her around the car and opened her door. "We're going to borrow this car for a short time and we're going to get somewhere safe."

Her eyes widened. "Borrow?"

"I promise I will make it right once your life isn't in danger."

She stared at him and then she nodded. "I trust that you will."

That was all Chandler needed. She trusted that he'd make it right, not just for the rental company, but for her. He would. He was bluffing his way through this, but so far he'd at least reacted decisively when the guy came to shoot them, twice now, and kept her safe. Sadly, his friend Ty was going to be in a mess when the police figured out whose car had a comatose hitman's body lying next to it.

But Ty would be more upset about the bullet holes in his baby.

Chapter Five

Chandler Delta had been Kylee's superstar crush for quite a few years, but being around him and watching him react so unwaveringly, bravely, and impressively to take out Creepy Eyes took him to an even higher level in her already too-infatuated mind.

He charmed the woman manning the gate, flirting with her and distracting her to the point that she waved him through without even thinking to look at their paperwork. It should've been impressive, but only confirmed what a ladies' man he was.

They got out of the airport without anything else crazy happening. They drove straight into downtown Boston, neither of them saying much, almost in silent agreement to wait to talk until they got somewhere safe. Chandler did call Papa, but he kept it short, telling him Kylee had found him, sharing the information she'd gleaned in a concise manner, telling him they'd borrowed a rental car, were headed into Boston, and did he know of any hotels downtown that would take cash without I.D.?

Papa took all the news stoically, promising he would intensify security around the secret and get the information into the right hands. He'd do all he could to stop Frederick from nuking the U.S. Then he cautioned them to be careful, said he'd find them a hotel or safe house in Boston soon, and hung up. Kylee could only imagine the mayhem at the Deltas' homes, but at least they had the information now and at least it sounded like Fredrick wouldn't proceed with his evil plans until he had the Delta weapon in hand. She'd keep praying Frederick's timeline didn't change and the Deltas could keep the secret weapon safe. The thought of America being hit by nuclear weapons was horrifying.

Chandler pulled into a Hertz rental car place and Kylee wondered if he was insane. "We'll be out of here in a second," he said confidently.

She hoped he was right. He parked the car in the line of returns, put two hundred-dollar bills in the cup holder, and then climbed out. Kylee followed his example, sliding out of her door as he came around to assist her. She had her purse, but her bag had been in her car back at the stadium and Chandler had left his large bag with the two lacrosse sticks hanging out of it in the Porsche. Were they going to hide out without even clean underwear? She rolled her eyes at herself. She was alive and Chandler was watching over her. That was all that mattered right now.

Oh, and praying Papa Delta's expertise and connections could stop Mimi and keep the United States from getting nuked.

It was a relief not to be carrying the burden of Mimi's secret conversation alone any longer, but sharing it also made it feel too real, as if the bombs were soaring through the sky toward them.

She looked up but could only see a crisp, blue sky over Boston's downtown section.

Chandler wrapped his arm around her and cuddled her against his chest. A thrill went through her and she forgot about the worries and stress for a moment. Even though she knew he was only trying to shelter her from any prying eyes, she savored the feel of him close.

They walked up to Quincy Market, the famous brick hall full of food places. Chandler led her around the outside of the building, where there were various street vendors selling tourist apparel. He quickly tucked a red Boston Redsox hat on her head and then bought her a white sweatshirt to match, helping her slide into it.

With her somewhat covered up, he wrapped her up close again and they walked to the southern end of the building. Unfortunately, they didn't stop to watch the street performers performing aerial tricks over the bald head of a man who flinched every time. The crowd was cheering and laughing, and she felt like it was almost a different world. She and Chandler were running from Mimi's or Frederick's man, or maybe men at this point. They could also be in trouble with the police or a rental car company enforcer. And overshadowing those minor concerns was the fact that the world might be about to end. It all felt surreal and crazy.

At the same time, being close to Chandler was as safe and yet thrilling as she'd felt since yesterday. No ... it was the safest she'd felt since her parents died and the most thrilling since the last time he held her close when they were only dumb, innocent teenagers with no clue how hard and lonely life could be. At least for her.

Chandler walked her into the middle of Quincy's market, tucking his sunglasses in his shirt. It would probably be more obvious to keep them on as the interior was much darker than outside with no windows and harsh overhead lights. The long corridor was busy and loud and delicious scents of greasy pizza, sweet breads, chocolate, and seafood all wrapped around her. She was starving, and then she saw the gelato. *Sim!*

"Are you hungry?" Chandler asked. "I'm starved. I usually eat right after my games to replenish my protein stores."

She looked up at him. His blue eyes still looked concerned, but he was obviously wanting to put her at ease.

"I figure we'll grab a few things and then hopefully Papa will have a place we can head for. We can eat and you can get some rest until Papa has an exit strategy for us."

"Thank you." She was enjoying this brief glimpse of how it would feel to be the woman Chandler Delta was not only taking care of but seemed to want to be with. They'd been thrown together because of Mimi's evil actions, but despite a lifetime of belittlement from her grandmother's mouth, Kylee might feel some gratitude for the woman if it brought Chandler back into her life.

That was hoping for too much. She wasn't a Chandler Delta kind of woman. This was only temporary, and she'd better keep her head on straight. She was grateful he was so kind and protective of her and she felt comfortable, safe, and thrilled to be with him just like she had as a sixteen-year-old.

All these feelings were one-sided, and she knew Chandler was an expert womanizer. Of course he'd make any woman feel like he was interested and make her feel safe and make her entire body tingle as he brushed his lips against her forehead before asking, "Dessert first? Cookies, pie, cake ... gelato? Now that's the ticket."

His eyes sparkled as if they weren't in danger but simply out on a fun adventure. "Let's get dessert and eat it while we explore all the food options. We can buy a bunch of food to take to the hotel and eat it family style so we can try different things. What do you think?"

She stared up at him. She thought she was in love with him. Could he honestly be that perfect? Dessert first? She hadn't had dessert first with anybody else since her dad had died.

He's out of your league, the snarky Mimi voice told her.

Tace, she commanded in Latin.

"I love gelato," she managed, probably sounding nothing like the brilliant linguist and teacher people claimed she was.

Just another reason you're fat.

Skáse, she begged in Greek.

She tried to ignore the voice. It came more often when she was tired and her defenses were down.

"Just another reason you're so perfect," he said, softly kissing her forehead and directing her to the closest gelato stand.

He was the perfect one. He'd devastated her at sixteen when he'd never texted or called, and she'd been too uncertain of herself to reach out first. Would she handle it any better as an adult when he went on his merry way dating models and influencers and being a superstar lacrosse player and she went back to her quiet life?

Kylee ordered the mint chocolate chip and Chandler got the mango. They savored their treats as they walked through the market. The gelato was absolutely delicious, and though Kylee should've been dissolving into a puddle of sweat and stress with the crazy turn her life had taken, she loved every bite.

Chandler asked her opinion on her favorite foods and then

bought everything she liked—a lobster roll, a poke bowl with every vegetable they had and searing the tuna instead of eating it raw, a calzone loaded with toppings, a bowl of clam chowder with sourdough bread, fish and chips, and a bunch of tropical juices. Chandler doubled up the bags and loaded the hot stuff in one and the cold in the other. He threw away his empty gelato cup and they listened with a crowd to an incredible violinist in the center plaza of the market while she finished hers.

She wasn't sure if they should be on the move, but she felt safe. Glancing up at her handsome bodyguard, she knew it was him that made her feel safe and like none of the ugliness of Mimi and Frederick could touch her.

Chandler pulled out his phone and read a text, then said, "Papa found a place." He directed her out the closest exit. They walked to the west and then north through the busy historic city, skirting the famous Boston Common.

Greeting the doorman of the hotel as if he were an old friend, Chandler escorted her into the XV Beacon. She felt instantly underdressed and like she really needed a shower as they entered the luxury hotel. The lobby was dark with wood paneling and white and red accents.

Chandler walked her to the front desk with all the confidence of a regular visiting dignitary. Despite the fact he was holding sacks of food and accompanying a disheveled woman in a baseball cap, too-large sweatshirt, knit skirt, and heels.

The classy front desk lady with a nametag of Madeline stood to greet them. Her gaze flicked over Kylee's attire, but she smiled warmly. "Hello and welcome to the XV Beacon. How can I help you?"

"Thank you, Madeline," Chandler said. "It's wonderful to meet you. I have a reservation under 'Superhero Status.'" He shook his head and laughed good-naturedly. "I'm assuming that was my brother's doing."

Her smile became even wider. "Your brother is quite charming."

"So I've been told. The guy thinks he's Thor."

They both laughed. That was funny, as Chandler's brother really was Thor or Thornton.

The woman clicked some buttons on her computer, scanned in key cards, slipped them into a paper holder, wrote on it, and handed everything over to Kylee since Chandler's hands were full.

"Thank you," Kylee said.

"My pleasure." She pointed to the room number she'd printed on the paper holder, 228. "Second floor. You can use the elevator or the stairs. We have a delicious steakhouse next to the lobby if you're hungry." Her gaze flicked to the food bags in Chandler's hands.

"We'll have to try that out tomorrow," Chandler said. "Do they offer breakfast?"

"Yes, and if you prefer, the room service menu is on the desk in the room."

"Perfect."

Kylee was itching to get into the room, take off her heels, eat, and then sleep, but she smiled and acted like nothing was amiss. Luckily, her skirt and summery blouse were both stretchy and comfortable, but she wished she'd been able to grab her bag from her car before she and Chandler took off from the stadium. Seeing Creepy Eyes shoot at them back at the stadium and then coming at Chandler's window with the gun made her not worry so much about not having clothes or moisturizer.

"Could you also send up whatever extra toiletries you have and some comfortable shorts for me and a T-shirt and yoga pants for my girl from your gift shop?" He looked tenderly at Kylee as if she really were "his girl," giving her heart palpitations. "I stole her away for this getaway and she wasn't prepared at all. I was too excited to be with her to think of anything else."

"Of course." The woman smiled as if they were the cutest couple she'd ever seen. "I'll have it all to you within the hour."

Kylee had to hand it to the lady. She was the consummate professional and if she thought it odd that she didn't know either of their names, they had only the clothes on their backs, or Chandler hadn't handed over I.D., she said nothing.

"Thank you." Chandler gave her a grin that made the woman blush and made Kylee wish she was the only one he grinned at like that. Silly thoughts.

They walked to the stairs and up. Kylee was feeling the exhaustion of the past twenty-four hours. Would she ever get back to her little apartment and visiting classes throughout the inner city, overseeing the language instruction of children from five to eighteen?

Stopping in front of door 228, Kylee scanned the card. It beeped, and she pressed the door handle down and pushed the door in. Chandler scooted into the room and held the door with his backside and that award-winning grin. Even with his hands full of bags, she was tempted to throw herself into his arms. They walked into a gorgeous white and dark wood suite, and she felt as if she'd been transferred into a fairytale. Maybe she never wanted to go back to that little apartment, though she would miss her kiddos.

There was a table with four chairs, a small kitchenette with gorgeous mahogany wood and white countertops, white couches with cozy-looking red throw blankets, and a huge four-poster mahogany bed with a fluffy white bedspread and a myriad of pillows. An open door to the right of the bed had to be the bathroom. Everything looked clean and fresh and luxurious and though it seemed like a spot of paradise, Kylee was suddenly hit with the awkwardness of being alone in a suite with the most handsome man in the world.

Chandler walked over and set the food bags on the table. "Are you ready to eat? I'm starving."

"Me too," she admitted. "I just need to use the restroom quick."

"Sounds good."

She hurried into the bathroom, which was also spacious and gleaming, mostly white with wood accents and red towels. Kylee looked longingly at the huge jetted tub. What she wouldn't give to soak and read her book. Yet being around Chandler felt like a real-life romance novel. With the craziness of what they were going through, she would probably categorize it as a romantic suspense. She loved being around him, but she was worn out from driving through the night and all the stress. She was afraid she would say or do something that she shouldn't because her guard was down.

She used the bathroom and then washed her hands, looking at her face in the mirror. Did Chandler really believe she was beautiful? Her parents had always told her how beautiful she was, but she assumed that was a parental duty. She'd received compliments and some interest from men and boys, but she kept to herself, avoiding any opportunities to meet men her age. In her experience, or at least what social media touted, most men were drawn to thin women, which she would never be. She'd tried every Keto, good belly, Paleo, no sugar, no carb diet known to man. All they did was make her miserable.

There was also the fact that Mimi had torn her down any chance she got. Why was it Kylee believed Mimi over her own parents? Those last two years of high school living with Mimi had been purgatory. Sometimes she wondered if she'd ever get the nasty Mimi thoughts out of her head. Shut up or be quiet in every language she knew hadn't worked yet.

She shook off the familiar stewing and applied lip gloss. Then she rubbed her scented coconut lotion on her neck and arms. A bath or shower would be better, but she didn't want to make Chandler wait, and she was hungry as well. She took the sweatshirt off, folded it and put it in the attached closet along with her purse and then unstrapped and slid off her heels. Ah. She wore heels almost every day, but it still felt wonderful to get them off.

Saying a quick prayer for strength to not throw herself at Chandler, she squared her shoulders. *Just eat and then get some sleep*, she begged herself. Tomorrow, hopefully Papa Delta would have worked his magic. Maybe dreams would come true and Mimi would get arrested, King Frederick would get shot, and she'd be back in her little apartment and going to work at the schools.

She opened the door and Chandler turned to her with a welcoming smile. He had the food and juices spread out on the table. "Dinner is served, beautiful lady."

Her heart took off at a gallop. What if her quiet apartment and

54

a good book and ice cream weren't the dream? What if Chandler Delta was the dream?

You'll never have Chandler.

Silenzio, she begged, but she knew. She felt it deep down. She was in so much danger—and it had nothing to do with a psychotic grandmother sending a hitman after her and an even more psychotic dictator with nuclear weapons aimed at her country.

Chandler Delta was trouble she had no idea how to stay away from.

Chapter Six

Chandler was almost dumbstruck by Kylee's beauty as she walked out of the bathroom in her fitted shirt and skirt, her lips and dark hair glistening and her long-lashed dark eyes seeming to be full of him. With her high heels off, she looked younger, smaller, and even more irresistibly innocent, making his protective instincts toward her even more intense. It didn't appear she was aware of the power she had over him or how beautiful she was.

He needed to keep his head on straight to protect her, as their nation's safety was at risk. Papa had called while she was in the bathroom, saying he had a plan that might involve Kylee, if she agreed, but to wait until he could do some more digging and talk to her in person. Papa sounded far too excited about the plan, which worried him. He also said he would have a chartered jet bring them to Colorado in the morning to keep her safe. She would be surrounded by his skilled and tough family until they decided which direction to go.

Chandler did not want her involved in any plan, but how did he go against an idea that could save hundreds of millions of lives and possibly thwart an evil dictator's progression of power? It was huge and honestly above his paygrade. He wanted to be the best Delta Protection Detail member he could, but truthfully he'd do better fighting someone with a lacrosse stick instead of a gun or knives.

He and Kylee settled down at the small table and ate the variety of delicious foods. He asked her questions about her work with the inner-city schools and overseeing foreign language classes for children from grade school through high school. Her favorite part was being involved in the teaching and she tried to be in the classroom as often as possible. It was impressive that as talented, smart, and beautiful as she was, she hadn't chosen the role of diplomat but tried to give back to the children.

The clothes and toiletries arrived as they finished eating and Kylee went to shower and change in the bathroom. Chandler spent the time pacing and checking in with his coaches. Luckily, they told him to take a few days for his "family emergency" and didn't ask questions. He doubted it'd only be a few days, but he'd cross that bridge when he got to it. He also replied to Ty's many upset texts about bullet holes in his baby and then Chandler deserting his Porsche. Apparently, the rental company had all kinds of questions Ty couldn't answer.

Chandler tried to humbly and profusely apologize, promising to pay any repair bill. Mostly he was just grateful it wasn't the police who were after his friend, or Creepy Eyes. He also stewed about the impending doom of the King Frederick situation and the worries over how to keep Kylee safe. He hated that Papa might ask her to go into a situation that was the opposite of safe to rescue the nation.

When she walked out of the bathroom for the second time that night, Chandler didn't know how it was possible for her to be even more beautiful, but there she was. He knew her beauty was enhanced for him because of how impressive, uplifting, and fun she was to be around and their connection from when they were younger. Despite her writing him off, he couldn't deny the strong feelings he'd kept in his heart.

Her face was clean and her hair was damp, shiny, and trailing over her shoulder. She was wearing the fitted T-shirt and yoga pants. Maybe the fact that the clothes were very, very tight was the reason his pulse skyrocketed and his palms started to sweat.

"Bathroom's all yours," she said, not quite meeting his gaze as if embarrassed by her body-hugging clothes. How did he tell her they were perfect on her?

"Thanks." Chandler strode toward her and couldn't resist brushing her arm with his and getting closer than he needed to.

She sucked in a breath and blinked up at him. She smelled clean and fresh. He loved how petite and feminine she was. His brother Thor had always thought she looked like Jennifer Lopez. Chandler could see the similarities, but he thought she was even more beautiful.

He leaned toward her, tempted like he had never been to steal a kiss without even properly dating her, and alone in a hotel room where the temptation to do more than kiss might prove his undoing. That went against what he'd been taught and the self-control he'd exercised with women his entire adult life.

Steeling himself, Chandler said a prayer for strength, nodded to her, and hurried into the bathroom. He'd already showered after the lacrosse game, so he washed his face, brushed his teeth, and changed into the simple cotton shorts they'd brought up. He eyed himself in the mirror, thinking he should probably put the T-shirt back on, but he'd never slept in anything besides underwear, so he figured the shorts were at least more modest than that. He'd never slept in the same hotel room as an unrelated female either, so there was that.

He walked out of the bathroom and stopped as he looked at the bed and Kylee's head peeking out of one side of it. She'd piled the many decorative pillows down the middle of the bed to form a barrier. Chandler laughed and asked, "To keep me on my side?"

"Yes, sir." She gave him an adorable grin. "I didn't want you to claim you needed to sleep on the couch."

He prowled toward her side of the bed even though he knew he shouldn't. "What makes you think I'd sleep on the couch?"

Her eyes widened and trailed over his chest. "Without the pillow barrier, either you're on the couch or I am, and I know what gentlemen you Delta boys are."

The reminder of being a Delta was one he needed, badly. "Good point."

Chandler pushed a hand through his hair and walked around the bed. Kneeling down, he said a prayer of gratitude for his and Kylee's protection and for heaven bringing her into his life again. He wondered if there was any chance of reconnecting like he'd hoped when he first saw her, but the danger surrounding them and the Delta secret were huge. He needed to push his selfish desires away.

Standing, Chandler looked over the pillow barrier at her small form in the bed, her dark hair and gorgeous tanned skin a beautiful contrast to the white bedding. She was turned away from him and her eyes were closed, but it was obvious by how quick she was breathing that she wasn't asleep and was feeling the tension in this room as surely as he was.

Was there really any harm in a goodnight kiss? The very thought of that had his body warming up and made him pant for air. If he walked around the bed, bent over, and simply gave her a pure but lingering kiss, would she slap him?

She probably should.

Instead of giving into his desires, he slid into the soft, cotton sheets. She let out the sweetest little gasp of air.

"You all right?" he asked.

"This is hard," she said quietly.

He rolled over and removed the two pillows blocking her face from his view. "Resisting all my charm is hard?"

She rolled over, took one of the pillows, and hit him in the face with it.

Chandler was very tempted to start a pillow fight but knew it wasn't smart. Instead, he laughed. "I guess I found a sensitive button."

"No, you didn't," she said primly. "Though I appreciate you rescuing me and think you are a great guy, and an even more impressive athlete, I am not one of your arm candy, post-pictures-of-us-all-over-social-media type of girls. I'm terribly sorry that I've upset your life and your ..." She paused, and Chandler wanted to tell her he was thrilled she showed up and he wasn't some display arm-candy girls type of guy, but she went on, "I'm sorry I've messed up your regular dating patterns, but I can't be some fill-in. Please, can you just … not treat me like your latest fling?"

"Oh," was his very articulate response. There was so much he wanted—needed—to say to all of that. How to get her to understand that women asked for pictures with him all the time and then they posted those pictures? He never wanted to be the jerk who told someone he wouldn't take a picture with them, but where the women posted and what they said was out of his control. Unless he wanted to make himself insane searching his own name online and correcting every fake claim.

She hit the button for the bedside lamps on the wall by the side of the bed and plunged the room into darkness. Now all he could hear was her breathing, which was still too fast and told him no matter how unhappy she seemed with him, she was affected by him. He wanted to say something, anything, but the moment had passed and he'd messed it all up.

Finally, he started with, "Kylee, you don't need to be jealous of the women who post pictures of me."

"*Pas du tout!*" Her exclamation of outrage filled the quiet room. "I am not jealous. You and I have no relationship, so who you date and what type of woman you like is no concern of mine."

Chandler thought it was a huge concern. Was she really not jealous? How could she say they had no relationship? Actually, from her perspective, she'd written him off at sixteen and that was that. She'd only come to him now because she was in a dark and desperate situation. Dang. He wished he knew how to say 'dang' in a different language.

"Once again, thank you for upsetting your life for me and protecting me. I appreciate your kindness. Goodnight."

He heard her roll over and could feel the angst radiating off of her. She was ticked at him but trying to show her appreciation at the same time. Chandler thought of himself as pretty laidback. He'd gotten into a few fights throughout the years and spent countless minutes in the penalty box, but he wasn't an out of control or contentious person. Right now, he felt himself getting more and more frustrated. She was the one who'd dumped him all those years ago because she was dating someone else, a boyfriend she'd conveniently forgotten while they were stealing kisses in the forest back home. Now she was upset at him because women posted pictures of him or because he dated like any adult male would? It was unfair, and it ticked him off.

He tried to put himself in her shoes. She was tired and probably irrational right now. Maybe in the morning they could talk reasonably about this. Maybe he could find out why she'd not only kissed him but connected so deeply with him as teenagers when she'd had a boyfriend back home. Maybe he was tired and irrational as well. Actually, that one was more than a maybe.

He rolled over and tried to fluff the pillow and settle down. He squeezed his eyes shut and tried to think of anything but the beauty in bed next to him, who was so appealing but didn't want him to flirt with her. This was looking to be a very, very long night.

Seconds ticked by like hours, and as he listened, her breath evened out. That was good. She needed sleep. They both did, but Kylee had to be exhausted from driving since last night and all the crazy stress surrounding her. It wasn't every day the fate of the free world rested on your shoulders.

He needed to focus on getting her to Papa and trying to help protect the Delta secret and Kylee. He was probably going to miss playoffs. That stunk. Especially as his team would suffer without him there and they'd been slated to take the championship this year.

Crazily enough, his lifelong passion with lacrosse seemed to pale in comparison to how consumed he was with the woman lying next to him. He wanted to roll over, shove the pillows away, take her in his arms, and show her exactly how much she should want to be his "latest fling."

That was wrong and Chandler wasn't the type to have meaningless flings with "arm candy." He wasn't some flirtatious player, though Kylee had obviously seen and believed the hype that he was. How to convince her otherwise? Kissing her would probably solidify her fears. Was she even interested in him like he was in her? He couldn't push her teenage rejection from his mind. It was silly, but it had been devastating to a sixteen-year-old boy who thought he'd found the love of his life.

When she'd appeared in the stands of his lacrosse game this afternoon, his sixteen-year-old self must've resurfaced, because he'd believed they would have their chance to be together forever like he used to dream about.

And apparently ... she wasn't into him and thought he was a heartbreaker and a jerk.

He punched his pillow and rolled over again.

The situation with King Frederik and the Delta secret should be his biggest worry, but all Chandler could think about was how taken he was with Kylee, and how she wasn't returning the feeling. This sucked.

Chapter Seven

Hours passed as Chandler tossed and turned, tempted by Kylee's soft exhalations and the picture of her in his mind. He wanted to push the pillows out of the way and gather her in his arms. How would she react to that? Probably not too well. Maybe she'd curse him in some foreign language. He'd forgotten to ask her what she'd said when they'd been shot at and the other times she'd said some phrase loudly. The different languages seemed to come out when she was upset. She was so irresistible. How to make her think he was the man she couldn't resist?

His eyes were finally growing heavy and he thanked heaven that he might drift off to sleep when a soft beep sounded. Chandler eased up in the bed and watched as their door handle turned. The exterior door slowly cracked open. A shaft of light from the hallway penetrated the darkened room.

Chandler's heart was suddenly racing for reasons that had nothing to do with Kylee's attractiveness and everything to do with her safety being in his capable but not as expert as his family members' hands. Any silly frustrations were shoved away, and he was grateful he hadn't fallen asleep.

His options now were to rush across the room and take the person out when they opened that door or he could fake being asleep and surprise the person. He didn't like option B as their assailant could shoot them both while Chandler laid in bed waiting to make his move.

A tool slid into the small opening and the person tried to manipulate the metal flip lock that Chandler had pushed over the door for added security.

He had a bit more time than he'd thought. He carefully slid out of the bed, picking up the pistol he'd set on the nightstand. Then he crept, he hoped quietly, toward the fireplace. He remembered seeing a fire poker over here. It was the best idea he had for a weapon that could incapacitate without a loud shot being fired. He wanted to take the person out but not kill them so he could get the information he needed. How had they been found again and who had sent the person?

He slid the 9mm he'd taken from Creepy Eyes into his shorts pocket and picked up the fire poker. Turning, he could see the guy was still messing with the door guard. At least he wasn't already in the room, and he didn't seem to have heard Chandler.

Edging to the wall, he worked his way silently along it until he was almost to the door. He could see the tool working and then the person finally flipped the catch out of the way. It clanged. Not loudly, but Chandler could feel the person freeze and wait to see if he'd woken either of them. Chandler didn't dare move either. He held his breath and prayed Kylee wouldn't wake and draw the invader's attention to her.

The door edged open and he could see a tall, bald man silhouetted from the hallway light. If he had to guess, it was Creepy Eyes. The guy edged in, staring at the bed and Kylee's silhouette. His right arm lifted, a pistol in his grip.

Any of his brothers would've pulled out their own pistol and shot the man, but Chandler was much more comfortable with a stick. He hefted the fire poker and brought it down fast and hard on the man's outstretched arm. Bone cracked, and the guy cried out in agony. The pistol dropped to the floor, luckily not discharging.

"Chandler?" Kylee cried out.

"Stay back," he cautioned.

Chandler was an expert at wielding a stick. He wasn't proud of all the time he'd spent in the penalty box over the years, but right now each of those penalties, and the clean hits he'd taken credit for over the years, served him well. He drew on the experience from lacrosse and from his dad, uncle, and grandpa training him, and the strength from working out hard every day. He wound up with the fire poker and slammed it with all his strength into the man's gut.

The guy crashed against the doorframe and then crumpled to the ground, gasping for air and whimpering in pain. Chandler thought the guy would live, but he might have internal injuries.

Holding on to the fire poker in case the guy got any ideas, or had more fight in him, Chandler grabbed the man by his good arm and yanked him into the room. He let the door fall closed behind him, released his grip, and pulled out the 9mm from his pocket.

This late at night, nobody had been in the hall and it didn't seem any of the other rooms had heard the fight. This high-dollar hotel was as soundproof as it was well built.

"Chandler?" Kylee asked again, her voice filled with panic.

He glanced at her and said, "Turn on a light, please. I think our friend Creepy Eyes found us again."

Kylee gasped and muttered, "*So ein sheil.*" The lamps and accents above the cabinets and planter shelves flipped on and she scrambled out of bed. She looked beautifully disheveled and Chandler would not let her get hurt. Ever. He had this weird swelling inside him. Kylee was his to protect and even if he wasn't an expert at protection like the rest of his family, he was proficient and he would give his life to keep her safe. The heaviness and intensity of that should've scared him. It didn't.

"Please stay back," Chandler cautioned. He didn't know what other weapons this guy had or if he'd rouse himself and fight again.

Kicking the man's weapon that he'd dropped over to the kitchen nook, Chandler pointed the pistol he'd acquired from this creep hours ago and said, "Now, tell us how you found us again."

The man gasped for air, holding his abdomen with his left hand, and wheezed out, "You ... I think I have internal injuries, and you ..." Another gasp for air. "... broke my wrist." He held his right hand up and his wrist did indeed look broken.

"That's the risk associated with being a criminal," Chandler told him, twirling the fire poker with his left hand. "I thought all you losers signed a disclosure."

"A disclosure?" the guy rasped out. He focused on the iron stick, genuine fear in his once chilly pale blue eyes.

"Yeah. When you committed to be a scumbag and attack innocent women, you signed a disclosure that your idiocy could result in death or dismemberment." Chandler was rewarded with a surprised laugh from Kylee and a recoiling from Creepy Eyes. The man tried to press himself against the wall, but he had nowhere to go.

"Now." Chandler leveled the pistol at him. "How did you find us?"

The guy rubbed at his abdomen, then cradled his broken wrist against it. His face was contorted in pain. Chandler should've felt worse about causing another human being agony, but this guy deserved it. This was the third time he'd come after them. Chandler knew this man was a professional or he couldn't have so easily tried to kill them. The clincher was him pointing his gun at the innocent Kylee while she slept. Any compassion Chandler might've felt had been wiped out by that coldness and threat to Kylee. It was pathetic that when the hitman got hurt, he reacted like a scared wuss.

"She has a ... tracker in her purse."

"Nope. We found that one back at the stadium. Try again."

His pale blue eyes narrowed, and he looked away. Tense seconds clicked by. Kylee's breath was coming too fast. Chandler wanted to comfort her and get her far from this loser and their compromised location, but that wouldn't help them until he knew how he'd followed them. Whoever had sent this guy could just send someone else. Hopefully there weren't other mercenaries on their way as Chandler wasted time with this loser.

Chandler took aim and swung the poker over the intruder's head, barely missing his bald pate and thumping into the wall, spraying plaster on the guy. The man cursed and ducked, curling into a ball. Chandler pushed the sharp metal tip into his chest, forcing him to straighten.

"Please don't hurt me again," the guy cried out.

"Tell me how you found us," Chandler snarled, wanting to make fun of this murderer for being such a wimp. It was always interesting how bullies couldn't take the tables being turned.

"Her necklace."

"*Nein!*" Kylee gasped and put a hand to her neck. She drew out a beautiful and probably expensive jade and diamond pendant. She must've always kept it hidden to protect the valuable jewelry. "Grandpa gave me this when my parents died." Her voice was quiet and sad.

Chandler's heart sunk on her behalf. She'd clung to the hope her grandpa was innocent. He knew she had. And to give her a meaningful gift when her parents died that had a tracking device in it? That was pretty sleazy.

She yanked it over her head and dropped it on a side table as if it were burning her.

He pushed the poker into the man's chest. "Is anyone else assigned to kill us?"

The man didn't hesitate. He shook his head. "Not yet. She had faith I could finish the job. I've never failed her before."

"She?" Chandler raised his eyebrows.

The man's lips thinned, but he obviously didn't want any more injuries. Chandler didn't enjoy hurting others, but he would do more damage if the guy didn't cooperate. He'd just admitted he'd planned to not just incapacitate them or slow them down. He'd been paid to kill them both, and he'd killed often enough his boss had complete faith in him.

"Olivet Seamons," he ground out.

Chandler looked at Kylee. She didn't look surprised, but she did look hurt. Maybe because her grandfather had given her the necklace that tracked her.

"You've been following Kylee since Chicago?"

The man nodded.

"Why didn't you kill her then?"

"She told me not to kill her unless she collaborated with someone. She didn't think she had anyone to turn to. When I saw her with you at the stadium, I knew it was time to finish the job."

"I hope you rot in Hades just like you deserve," Chandler said.

The guy simply raised his eyebrows. Obviously killing an innocent woman was nothing to him.

"Kylee," Chandler said softly. "Can you bring me my phone, and then if you're comfortable, would you pick up his gun and point it at him? If he moves, shoot him through his black heart."

"Gladly," Kylee said, a lot more spunk in her voice than Chandler had planned on. Good girl. She grabbed Chandler's phone and brought it to him. He set the poker on a nearby entry table and took the phone with his left hand. He waited until Kylee picked up the man's other pistol, walked up closer, and pointed it at him. Her hands shook, but only slightly. She was far enough back that the man couldn't touch her, but a shot at that range wouldn't miss.

"You're so impressive," Chandler told her.

She smiled. "I'd happily shoot this jerk who tried to kill us twice earlier today and was willing to murder us while we slept."

Chandler didn't know if she really would shoot, but he was proud of her spunk. He traded his pistol to his left hand and his phone to his right. He hit Papa's number with his finger. Cradling the phone in his neck, he transferred the pistol back to his right hand. The guy didn't attempt to move. His hand and the hit to his abdomen must've been hurting him really bad, or maybe two guns pointed at him and the fact that he'd just given away his employer's name told him he had failed. Maybe Olivet Seamons was so evil the man would rather be imprisoned than deal with her repercussions.

"Chandler?" Papa's voice was rough as if he was sleeping, but he sounded fully awake. "You okay?"

"I just took out the man who tried to shoot us twice and has been following us. He broke into our hotel room. Can you send someone you trust to apprehend and interrogate him? He somehow got away from the police at the airport car rental." Chandler raised an eyebrow to the man on the floor.

"I hid under a car and waited until they gave up searching." The man looked proud that he'd done something right.

"I'm on it," Papa said. "Do you know how he tracked you?"

"We do now. I'll take care of the tracker and get Kylee someplace safe until the plane is ready."

"I'll see if I can accelerate the plane's departure. I'll be in touch. Good job."

"Thanks." Chandler hung up and smiled at Kylee. "Papa's sending someone, then we can get away from this filth."

"I'm looking forward to that," she said.

Her radiant smile stole the oxygen from his lungs. She should be quivering under the covers crying with all she'd been through, but here she was smiling and impressing him even more. If only she wanted to date him like he did her.

Chandler sensed movement. He turned as the guy pushed off the floor with his good hand and crouched as if to spring. Chandler swept the poker off the floor, dropping his gun while he was still down low. He swung into the movement like he was chopping wood at an angle. The metal iron collided with man's head as he leaped forward. Chandler felt the contact all the way through his arms. The guy went down in a heap, and he didn't move.

Chandler pushed the hitman over onto his back. His eyes were closed, but his chest was moving up and down. He bent down low and put his hand to the guy's nose. Creepy Eyes was breathing.

Straightening, he looked at Kylee. Her eyes were wide, and she clung to the gun. "Sorry," she squeaked. "I said I'd shoot, but I didn't even react. You reacted, though. You're more than a lacrosse superstar, aren't you?"

Chandler chuckled. It was nice she knew more than most people did about his family and their training, but she had no idea the full extent.

"I'd much rather be playing lacrosse than fighting with a fire poker," he told her.

She grinned. "Well, you look great doing either."

His chest warmed and the appreciation in her dark eyes stoked that warmth into a flame. He didn't like hurting someone with a fire poker, but somehow it had brought the sparkle back into Kylee's eyes. Maybe she wasn't interested in him and thought he was a playboy, but then again ... maybe she was interested and if he could put her fears of him being a heartbreaker to rest, they might have a chance.

He had at least the next few days to get through to her. The world's safety was hanging in the balance. Chandler was too focused on the dark-eyed beauty smiling at him to worry overly much about anything else. Thankfully, Papa and his family would worry enough to make up for him being distracted.

Chapter Eight

Kylee was so worn out by the time they talked to the investigator, gathered their things, waited for an Uber, drove to a small commuter airport, and waited in a plush executive hangar for their chartered plane to arrive that she could hardly function. Chandler stayed right by her side and was kind and attentive. He was some kind of superhero in her book. She still hated that he was a womanizing charmer, but she could completely understand how no woman could resist him and those blue eyes of his. He protected her like he was an expert military man with a fire poker, looked incredibly handsome doing it, and treated her as if she was the only woman in the world. She knew the last one wasn't true, though, and she wasn't going to open her heart to him again only to have him promise to text and call and never follow through. But she could sure appreciate him.

Chandler escorted her up the steps of the small jet. It had seats up front for the co-pilot and pilot and then eight plush burgundy seats lined up two by two in the back.

The pilot explained the small bathroom and how the toilet worked and then returned to his pre-flight checklist. Kylee sank into a chair, tightened her seat belt, told Chandler thank you, and was asleep before they left the ground.

A hand on her arm stirred her. She looked into those brilliantly blue eyes and was lost to anything but Chandler Delta.

"Hey," he said softly, his gaze roving over her face as if he was more taken with her than she was with him. That was ridiculous. No wonder women went gaga over him. Not only was he a superstar, but the way he made her feel with one touch or glance was off the charts. How could she keep resisting him?

"Hey," she repeated, straightening and hoping she hadn't drooled. "We almost there?"

"Yeah. We're landing outside of Denver. It's a couple hours' drive to our valley."

"I remember," she said.

His eyebrows rose and his gaze deepened. Flashbacks of laughing and teasing with him and then sneaking into the forest to kiss hit her like that fire poker. She gasped for air.

"How much do you remember?" he asked softly.

Kylee took a fortifying breath, praying for strength. She looked away from his eyes and out the window. The land was flat to the east but stretched to the mountains west of Denver. It had surprised her last time she came here how the city of Denver was flat and everything east of that looked like Kansas but to the west those glorious, green mountains offered sanctuary, excitement, and ... she chanced a glance at Chandler ... a life she could never live.

"I remember how pretty your valley was." She tried to evade what he was really asking. Of course she remembered ... them. He'd quickly become her everything, and then he'd just as quickly forgotten her.

"I've never forgotten how pretty you are."

Is he blind?

Tumahimik ka, Mimi. Maybe Tagalog would work.

His gaze traveled over her and stoked the flame that threatened to take over her entire being if she didn't fight it. He was the type that complimented every girl. She wasn't special to him. He was only trying so hard because she wasn't flinging herself against his perfect chest and begging him to kiss and love her. She was a challenge for the player, and he'd be gone the second after she gave in. She had to stay away from his arms and especially his lips. Though it was tempting to give in and kiss him, to at least have some wonderful memories as she grew old alone with her ice cream and novels.

"What time is it?" she asked.

"A little after two."

"Did you sleep?" she asked, trying to sound chipper. "You definitely deserved a rest after taking Creepy Eyes out for good."

His eyes narrowed at her redirection, but he nodded. "I slept."

The plane swooped down and she watched out the window as they landed smoothly on an asphalt runway. Large airport hangars and numerous small airplanes were scattered throughout the private airport.

She undid her seatbelt and stood to stretch as soon as the plane taxied to a stop. Feeling Chandler's gaze on her, she looked over at him. He also stood but was staring almost broodily at her. His gaze pleaded with her to share her innermost thoughts and to fall desperately for him like any woman would want to do. He was an expert with those eyes of his, maybe even better at entrancing women than he was on the lacrosse field or disabling bad guys with fire pokers.

She looked away and was relieved when the pilot hurried down the aisle and opened the plane door for them.

"Thank you," she and Chandler said at the same time.

She laughed nervously.

"My pleasure," the man said. He gestured them off, then hurried back to his cockpit.

She slung her purse over her shoulder and Chandler took her elbow and escorted her off the plane. They'd waited forever for the investigator to come last night and then they'd hurried out of there. She should've thought to change, but she'd been pretty distracted, so she still had on the far too tight T-shirt and yoga pants and her high-heeled sandals. She hadn't had a chance to do her hair and had no makeup on. Talk about the worst way to see Chandler's family for the first time in years.

She reached for her necklace under her shirt to give her strength like she often did. Then she remembered it was gone. Chandler had given it to a homeless mother and told her it was real and she could sell it. The woman had been overjoyed. Kylee was glad the necklace could help someone, but sorrow traced through her and she felt the last connection to her family snap.

How could her grandpa be as evil as Mimi? The raw edges of the frayed connection were painful and sharp, poking at her soul and taking away any confidence her grandfather had instilled in her.

Forcing a smile on her face, she walked off the plane to greet Chandler's family. As luck would have it, waiting for them were his classy and beautiful parents and a younger couple. The man was Chandler's older brother, one of the twins, and almost as handsome as Chandler. His girlfriend or wife was the most exotically gorgeous and thin woman Kylee had ever seen. The lady had creamy brown skin, long, dark hair, and sparkling brown eyes. She somehow had a well-defined chest and hips despite how thin she was. Not fair. And of course she was dressed in a gorgeous off-white button-down dress with a brown belt that emphasized her small waist.

Kylee batted away the jealousy. It was not this woman's fault that she was model gorgeous, and no matter how easy it was to feel the ugly jealousy, it wouldn't do anything for Kylee to be petty and envious.

She pasted on her smile and walked down the steps and into Myrna Delta's open arms. It felt like, for just a moment, her mom had come back. Kylee immediately sank into the hug. She was clinging. She was crumpled against Chandler's mom, surprised by the fifty-something woman's strength. Myrna didn't seem to care, and nobody else said anything.

After a few wonderful moments, Myrna pulled back slightly and framed Kylee's face with her hands. "It's been too long, sweetheart. We begged the Admiral to let you come visit, but ..." she trailed off and forced a smile.

Kylee could only imagine Mimi would never have let her come back to visit once they had custody of her. She'd never heard anything about it.

"Let me get a proper look at you now," Myrna continued. Her gaze trailed fondly over Kylee's face, like the favorite aunt that Kylee never had. "Oh, my, goodness! For heaven's sake, you are even more gorgeous now than you were as a teenager."

"Um ... thank you," Kylee managed, not buying Myrna's kind words but appreciating them all the same. She snuck a glance at Chandler and his gaze said he agreed with his mom and wished she'd give him a chance. She quickly looked back at Myrna but could see in the woman's green eyes that she'd noticed the look she and Chandler shared, and she was scheming. *Ach, nein.* It was hard enough to resist Chandler's charm without his amazing mother matchmaking them.

"It's wonderful to have you here," Myrna continued. "Even though it's not ideal circumstances."

"Thank you," was all she could think to say again.

Myrna released her to hug her son and Keith Delta gathered her into a daddy hug that made tears sting the corners of her eyes. "Don't worry, Kylee," he said softly. "You're safe now. I'm grateful you were inspired to go to Chandler."

Once again, Kylee's gaze was yanked to her protector's handsome face. "Me too," she admitted, making his eyes light up. Protector. She had to think of him as that. He was an impressive, kind, and amazing man, but soon the time in this picturesque valley with this model-perfect, brilliant, but somehow ultra-accepting family would be done. She'd be back working at the schools. With her grandfather betraying her, she'd be truly alone. That is, if King Frederick didn't succeed and bomb America with nuclear weapons. Why did nuclear winter sound less scary than being alone? Maybe because she'd be in heaven with her parents and that sounded pretty amazing, actually.

She released Keith and turned to Chandler's brother while Chandler still hugged his mom.

The handsome man gave her a quick hug and said, "It's good to see you, Kylee."

"You too ... Thor?"

Everyone but the brother laughed. He gave her an injured look and said, "Please ... you can't think I'm the ugly twin. I'm Aiden."

"Sorry." She laughed too, seeing the teasing in his eyes. She'd almost forgotten how the twins razzed each other and Chandler and Hudson nonstop. They all treated their older sister Esther with the utmost respect and nobody messed with the brother Greer too much, the quiet, tall cowboy. Though she'd seen Greer get in a wrestling match with them from time to time. "I can definitely see the difference now. You're the handsome one. The Navy SEAL. Aiden."

"Thank you very much." He winked. "And this is my gorgeous fiancée ... the only woman pretty enough to be my equal in looks, and benevolent enough to put up with me," he lowered his voice for the last line, "Melene Collier."

Everybody laughed at that. Melene shoved Aiden playfully and then turned to Kylee with a radiant smile. Gorgeous was right. Kylee felt inferior, but that was on her own lack of self-confidence. There was no way to resist Melene's warmth, especially as she enfolded Kylee in a hug and said, "I'm so glad you're safe and Chandler rescued you. Sometime, I'll have to share the story of how Aquaman saved me." She winked at her fiancé.

Aiden brushed his hand over his hair and grinned. "I'm Aquaman." He gave Chandler a challenging look. "What's your nickname?"

Chandler rolled his eyes at the jab.

"Lacrosse superstar who can take out evil men with fire pokers," Kylee rushed to say. "Sorry it's not concise. I'm working on a better one. Maybe *el campéon*. That's champion in Spanish."

She was rewarded with a grateful smile from Chandler. There was something in his eyes that hit her deep in the gut. Was the superstar not as confident in some areas of his life? Maybe his "Aquaman" brother with the sweet, gorgeous fiancée made him feel a little inferior as well. She'd have to ponder on that because it didn't make sense. She'd seen Chandler cuddled up in pictures with women every bit as gorgeous as his future sister-in-law. Maybe everybody in the world felt inferior in some way. They were just better at hiding it than she was.

"Well, let's get you two home," Myrna said brightly. She took Kylee's arm and directed her toward a black Chevy Suburban. "Do you have a bag, sweetheart?"

Kylee shook her head. "If I had a bag, I can promise you I wouldn't be wearing these skintight clothes paired with heels." She smiled and hoped that hadn't come across too bratty.

Myrna laughed and Melene's tinkling laughter joined her future mother-in-law's. Kylee was sandwiched between the two women as they walked. The men had fallen back a few steps and were discussing something intensely. Probably the future of their nation. Kylee was so relieved to push the heaviness of the secret she'd carried for less than twenty-four hours onto the Delta family's capable shoulders.

"If I had a body like yours, I'd wear too-tight clothes every day," Myrna said.

Melene nodded her agreement. "You look incredible," the picture-perfect model added. "Little wonder Chandler can't stop staring." She winked.

Kylee could only blink at them. Were they both insane, did they enjoy lying, were they blind, or were they simply the kindest women on the planet? "Um ... thank you?"

Myrna studied her deeply as only a mother could do as they reached the Suburban and waited for the men who were plodding toward them, Chandler speaking rapidly as if conveying a mountain of information in mere seconds. "Do you know how gorgeous you are?"

Pathetic lying.

Sei ruhig!

Kylee shifted uncomfortably under Myrna's gaze. Thankfully, the men reached them before Myrna could demand an answer, though Kylee had the feeling this wasn't the end of the conversation.

They all loaded into the Suburban. Keith and Myrna were up front, Chandler and Kylee in the middle bucket seats, and Melene and Aiden cuddled in the smaller backseat. Kylee offered to climb in the back as her legs were much shorter than Aiden's, but he smilingly told her he wouldn't pass up the chance to cuddle his future wife. Even if he got leg cramps.

She was jealous of more than Melene's beauty as the two of them looked to be head over heels in love. Would she ever find that? Not when she compared every man to her teenage crush. The teenage crush who'd ghosted her, but was currently sitting close by, looking far too appealing.

Keith and Aiden immediately started drilling Chandler with questions. They also questioned Kylee, albeit a little less intensely. They both shared everything they could about what she'd overheard, what had happened to them, and then she tried to share everything she could think of about her grandparents and their numerous business and social associations. She didn't have as much info as they'd like as she avoided going home as much as possible, but they all agreed it was curious how much money Mimi flaunted when they knew exactly what the Admiral's salary was. It was a great salary, but it probably wouldn't allow them to live in a five-million dollar house and travel the continent in private jets staying at luxury resorts.

The conversation finally shifted focus away from Kylee as she was able to draw out Melene and Aiden's story. They told an insane tale of King Frederick's right-hand man, General Carl Phillip, putting a million-dollar bounty on Melene's head after Aiden rescued her like a real-life Aquaman, their escape from mercenaries in Jamaica, Phillip faking his death, and then pursuing her to the Deltas' valley to get the Delta secret. It all made complete sense, no matter how crazy it was, because it played right into King Frederick's goals. She'd heard General Phillip had died in friendly fire. Aiden was happy to tell her they were certain he would stay dead now.

Aiden and Melene had just flown in as well, from Costa Rica

where Melene was a coordinator for Avalyn Shaman-Hawk's charitable organization Health for All. Sheesh. Could the woman be any more perfect?

Apparently Aiden and Melene had come home to help protect the secret, though he was trying to lobby for Papa to use his connections and allow Aiden and his fellow SEAL Team 8 to go on a covert op and take out King Frederick. Myrna did not like that idea at all, and Melene agreed. Kylee would hate for Aiden and his friends to be in danger, but it would prevent so much death if they could take King Frederick down. Even if he didn't use nuclear weapons, he was killing many innocent people.

They explained Papa had a special assignment for their cousin Maddie so she wouldn't be home for a few more weeks and unfortunately they couldn't get ahold of Hudson right now as he was filming somewhere in the mountains of Peru and his producers kept promising to get the message to him to call home, but either he was ignoring it or they weren't giving it to him. Kylee got the sense that Hudson was even more of a carefree, crazy man than he'd been as a young teen. Myrna seemed sad he wasn't home yet, but the rest of them didn't seem surprised by it. He had come home for Thor's wedding, but hadn't stayed long.

The rest of the Delta family was in the valley and diligently working to keep any of King Frederick's cohorts from finding the secret. If necessary, they would not only call in Aiden's SEAL teammates but some other special ops forces too. The problem was they wanted to keep the secret... well, secret. So the fewer people who knew about it, the better.

They drove through gorgeous mountain scenery and finally passed through the picturesque Summit Valley before heading up the narrow canyon to the Deltas' very own valley. Kylee sighed audibly when she saw the too-blue lake, the high, green mountains, and the gorgeous houses. There was a newer house, barn, and corral about half a mile around the side of the lake that they explained was Greer's. Melene pointed toward the trees and told her Thor, Alivia, and Colton all had homes up in the trees. Alivia and her fiancé Klein had built all the recent homes and updated Papa's, Myrna and Keith's, and Holly and Joseph's homes.

How would it be to live in such an ideal spot, surrounded by not only nature's beauty but numerous family members who loved you and had your back? Kylee's only family were Grandpa and Mimi, and apparently they both hated her. She reached for her necklace again, only to find her neck bare. Swallowing back the emotion, she could hardly believe the jade necklace she'd worn since her parents passed was actually a tracking device. If she saw her grandfather, she would scream at him. She'd always thought he was on her side. The hurt was deep and raw.

They unloaded from the vehicle and a small crowd of people hurried down the porch steps to greet them—Papa Delta along with Aiden's twin Thor, Chandler's Aunt Holly and Uncle Joseph, and his cousin Colton and a beautiful brunette. If she remembered right, this was Papa's house.

Everybody started hugging each other and Kylee as well. She should've felt like an outsider at this family reunion, but they all were far too inclusive. They explained everyone else was either at work, patrolling to protect the secret, or watching monitors and she would see them soon. She met Colton's girlfriend Bailey, who was also from Chicago, and they got chatting about favorite places to eat and trails to walk.

"Come inside." Papa gestured. "I'm sure you're all starving. We saved lunch." He looked at Kylee. "You and Chandler will stay here with me, and Aiden and Melene will stay with Joseph and Myrna. Do you have a bag, my dear?"

Kylee shook her head. "If I had a bag, I wouldn't be dressed like this." She gestured to herself and made the mistake of glancing at Chandler. His gaze was hot on her and made her eyes widen. She involuntarily stepped back, running into his dad.

Everyone else laughed as Bailey and Melene both assured her she looked great.

"No worries, sweetie," Myrna said. "We've got plenty of clothes and toiletries. We'll get a bunch together and bring them to your room."

"Thank you."

They walked into Papa's spacious living area, sat around the table and the huge bar, and ate a creamy potato and veggie soup and Monte Cristo sandwiches with the best raspberry jelly she'd ever had as Kylee and Chandler repeated their story again. Kylee was getting tired of telling it, but she pushed that selfish thought away. This was a huge deal and these people were going to protect her nation against a depraved lunatic. She could at the very least share any detail she could think of. Papa seemed very disturbed by her grandpa being the one who'd given her the jade necklace. He'd obviously hoped it was all Mimi too.

They finished eating, cleaned up, and Papa Delta said, "Now, we'll keep brainstorming and have a family meeting with everyone not on duty tonight after dinner. Kylee and Chandler, would you both like to get settled in your rooms and take a nap? You both look exhausted, and we need you fresh to discuss our plans to stop Frederick."

Kylee appreciated his kindness, but her face flushed. Great. Not only were her clothes skin tight, but she also looked exhausted.

"Sure," Chandler said.

She nodded.

"I'll show her the guest rooms," Chandler offered.

"We'll get some clothes and toiletries together for you," Myrna reaffirmed.

None of their clothes are going to fit you.

Bud' spokoyen. She didn't know much in Russian, but of course she'd learned "be quiet". She hoped it would somehow shut down the hateful voice someday, but maybe she needed to come up with a different strategy.

"Thank you." Kylee looked around the room, ignoring the Mimi jab. These people were all far too good-looking, smart, and tough for anybody's good, but they didn't act like they were better than her. Unlike Mimi and her circle of friends, the Deltas seemed intent on building Kylee up and being far too kind. They were impressive in so many ways, most of all Chandler, but she had to keep her distance from him and shield her heart.

"Thank you for taking me in and taking this weight off my shoulders," she said, looking around the room. "I was so terrified when I overheard Mimi and that man, but I knew if anyone could save the world, it would be the Delta family." She'd learned that from her grandfather. She was questioning a lot about Grandpa Seamons right now, but she thought he was dead-on about how brilliant and remarkable the Deltas were.

Most of them smiled graciously, but Thor pushed his hand through the air. "Oh, go on. You'll give me a big head."

"Too late," Aiden said.

"I'll give you a sore head." Thor sprang at his twin, ripping him away from Melene.

They started wrestling right there in the living room. Nobody seemed to find that odd at all, and Joseph and Keith each chose a twin and started placing bets and cheering for them.

Chandler ignored them and walked up to her. "Sorry. We can't take them anywhere."

His mom laughed. "Boys, right?" She bustled off toward the back door. "I'm going to gather the perfect clothes for that gorgeous shape of yours," she said to Kylee with a wink.

Kylee waved a hand, her cheeks hot. Gorgeous shape? Maybe all these people preferred an excess of bust and hips. If she asked, would one of J. Lo's movies and Beyonce's songs be their favorites as well?

Chandler gestured her toward the front entry. She stood from her barstool and walked with him. As they started up the grand staircase, he explained, "Papa's master bedroom is on the main level and downstairs we have rooms for Delta Protection Detail purposes. You'll probably see those when we brainstorm tonight. Up here, there are four guest suites. You can have your pick."

They reached the top of the stairs and she poked her head in the first door. It was beautiful with wide windows showcasing the lake and mountains, a dresser and comfortable-looking leather armchair and footrest, and a large bed with a soft-looking comforter and pillows. An open door revealed a bathroom with a tile floor and a marble counter.

"It's a beautiful house," she said, turning back to face him.

He nodded. "It is." Chandler eased closer, and she leaned against the doorframe for support. He put his hand on the wood frame next to her and looked her over. "My mom is right, you know."

"About?"

"You are absolutely gorgeous."

She didn't think his mom had phrased it that way, but she loved that Chandler had. She wanted to protest that she wasn't, but she could see in his blue eyes ... he thought she was gorgeous.

She blinked up at him, forgetting that she needed a shower and clean clothes, a nap, and the world to not be threatened by an evil dictator and her more evil grandmother. She leaned up toward him, thrills filling her as he wrapped his arms around her waist and pulled her tight to his muscular body. She easily forgot that he could break her heart just as quick as he could pull her to him.

"You are also smart and very brave," Chandler said in a husky tone that shot desire through her.

"Thank you, Chandler," she whispered, wrapping her arms around his neck and tugging his handsome face down closer to hers.

"You believe me?" he asked earnestly.

"That I'm smart, brave, and ..." she almost choked on the word, "gorgeous?"

He nodded, his blue eyes intense, begging her to believe him.

It hit Kylee harder than that fire poker had taken out Creepy Eyes. This charm and Delta quality that Chandler had ... it was why so many women fell for him, were obsessed with him, and fought for a date or picture with him. His family were all great at making a person feel special, but Chandler took it to the next level and somehow hypnotized every woman to feel important and beautiful to him. The power in his blue eyes alone took her breath away. Add to that his handsome face, well-built body, ability to protect her, and superstar lacrosse abilities... He was irresistible, and he was right about one thing. She *was* smart. Too smart to go down this heartbreak trail again.

She released her grip on him and tried to dodge into the bedroom, but she didn't move. Chandler hadn't released his grip on her. There was no world where she could get free from him if he didn't want her to.

"Kylee?" his voice was full of surprise. She could bet no woman had ever refused Chandler Delta when he went for a kiss.

"I'm exhausted," she managed, far too tired to handle inquiries from him about if she could believe she was 'gorgeous' and why she should fall for, kiss, and date him like any woman would yearn to do. Yet Kylee had taken this route before, and the aftermath still hurt. She was smart enough to avoid ripping scabs off of wounds that should have been fully healed long ago.

"Okay." He nodded but didn't look convinced. Thankfully, he released her.

She scurried into the room, shut the door, and leaned against it, releasing and pulling in quick breaths. She had no idea how she would keep resisting him. Hopefully Papa's plan involved Kylee traveling to some foreign shore and fighting King Frederick.

You're a laughingstock. No way would he send the person with the least amount of skills and fighting experience.

Joyonghi hae!

She plodded to the bathroom. Her life was like a living nightmare, with Mimi's voice in her head capping off the horrific experience.

Except Chandler was no nightmare. He was perfection in a manly shell. He was also a heartbreaker of epic proportions. How to keep that forefront in her mind?

Chapter Nine

Chandler waited by Kylee's door for a few beats, but obviously she wasn't going to fling it open and kiss him. He'd been moments away from her lips meeting his. She'd actually been arching up to him. Then he'd complimented her and it had thrown her for a loop. Dang it.

He yanked out his phone and Googled "dang it" in French. *Bon sang.* He could remember that. *Bon sang!* Then he Googled beautiful in a few languages: *belle, hermosa, bellissima, and linda* were the ones he thought he could remember from French, Spanish, Italian, and Portuguese. He'd probably say them all wrong, but maybe it would somehow touch Kylee. He had no idea how to get through to her how deeply he cared and how beautiful he thought she was from the inside out.

Who had damaged her and how could she not internalize how appealing and impressive she was? She wasn't just gorgeous physically but emotionally, mentally, and spiritually too. Kylee was the complete package to him, and somehow he couldn't convince her of that. Was it because of his playboy reputation, had someone hurt her deeply, or was he simply lacking what a brilliant and impressive woman like Kylee would want in a man?

He pushed out a disgruntled breath and went into the bedroom next to Kylee's. After taking a long shower, he lay down. He thought he'd stew and toss and turn, but it seemed he'd barely closed his eyes when somebody jostled his shoulder.

"Come on, lacrosse superstar who can best a bad guy with a fire poker or was it *el campéon*?" Aiden's voice was far too close, and the room was too dark to see him clearly. Night must've fallen while he slept.

Chandler took a swing at where the voice had come from and connected with Aiden's chest instead of his jaw.

"Oh, little bro is ready to rumble." Aiden jumped onto the bed and started hitting him.

Chandler wasted no time punching back. They rolled around on the bed laughing and trading hits and trying to overpower each other until the bedroom light flicked on and then his mom's voice came from the doorway. "Oh my goodness, are you boys ever going to outgrow insulting and pummeling each other?"

Aiden got in one more cheap shot, then jumped up and strode to where their mom leaned against the doorframe, shaking her head at them, a patient smile on her lips.

"Where would be the fun in that, beautiful Mama?" He bent down and kissed her on the forehead.

"Maybe save me a few gray hairs," their mom said.

Aiden only laughed, knowing not to touch that with a ten-foot pole. Their mom and Aunt Holly both colored their hair and were beautiful ladies. They all knew it was the danger surrounding their families that stressed their moms out. At the same time, their moms were as well trained as any of them and had helped train their own children. No matter how prepared the entire family was, it had to be hard on a parent, especially a mom, to allow her children to be in dangerous situations.

"You still fight pretty well, for a lacrosse player," Aiden shot at him.

"I can at least best a Navy SEAL," Chandler hurled at his back.

Aiden laughed and walked out of the room.

Chandler knew it wasn't true. Aiden could thump him with one hand tied behind his back. But at least Chandler could keep taunting him. He sat up, still feeling worn out.

His mom came and sat down on the side of the bed. "How are you really, love?"

Chandler smiled at her. "I'm doing great. We're headed to the playoffs, as long as I don't get benched for missing practice."

"I'm sorry you're missing practice, and even more sorry that we've missed the last few games."

"It's fine, Mama."

"It's not." Her green eyes turned as fierce as he'd ever seen them. "You know I've never missed a game until this fall."

"I know." His mom was as loyal to the Deltas and the secret as any of them, but missing an event for one of her children ranked up there with missing church on Sunday. It wasn't done unless you were on your death bed. He wouldn't put it past her to go take King Frederick out herself and eliminate the threat to her family and never miss another lacrosse game. She even tried to get to as many of Hudson's crazy stunts in person as she could. It was tough as he performed often and usually in faraway locales. They all adored their little brother, but he had distanced himself from the family, even his parents. It was hard to understand or watch. Even though Chandler and Aiden didn't live close, they tried to keep in contact with FaceTime, phone calls, and texts.

"At least you got to watch this handsome guy on television."

"That is some consolation." She looked him over. "I was thrilled that Kylee felt impressed to come to you."

"Yeah." He nodded. She'd shared that part of the story with everyone in the Suburban, but he hadn't heard it before then.

"How has it been ... reconnecting?"

Chandler knew she was digging, but he didn't want to admit it wasn't going the direction he hoped and have his mom start dropping heavy hints to Kylee. He wanted to win her affections like a man. "Is she still resting?" he asked.

"No." Her eyes reflected frustration at his lack of answer. "I woke her up when I took her all the clothes and toiletries. She's helping make side dishes for dinner with Shelly and Thor."

He nodded. He was excited to see Shelly. His brother's cowgirl was feisty and fun to be around.

His mom looked him over. "It was a shame to have her change out of that T-shirt and those yoga pants."

"Mama," he reprimanded her. "You need to stop."

"Oh!" She shoved at his arm. "You all can tease nonstop, but I get in on it and I have to stop?"

"Tease me all you want." Chandler tried to give her a stern

look. "But you'll embarrass Kylee. I want her to feel comfortable here and I sense she's not ... confident about her shape."

His mom instantly looked repentant. "You're right, and I've worried about the same thing." She heaved out a sigh. "I can't imagine how she's dealt with not only losing her parents but going through her last couple years of high school in Olivet's custody, enduring that woman's petty jealousy and, I'm sure, poisonous jabs. To think that snotty, traitor of a woman and Admiral Seamons are the only family Kylee has left." Her shoulders rounded. "It hit her hard that her grandpa was the one who gave her that necklace."

He nodded. "For sure. I told her I could take the tracker out and she could keep it, but she wanted nothing to do with it." He wanted to be careful not to encourage the matchmaker, but he needed some advice from his smart mother. "How do we help her feel good about herself?"

"We can keep giving her compliments and try to open her eyes to her beauty both inside and out, but it's going to be hard to overcome years of that viper's poison."

Chandler winced. He hated that for Kylee. He hated that her grandmother had not only belittled her but now betrayed her as well, and to top it off, actually tried to kill her only grandchild. It was hard to wrap his mind around. Was Kylee's emotional abuse at her grandmother's tongue and her inability to see how incredible she was part of her rejection of him? Or was he simply looking for a reason besides the fact she just wasn't interested?

"Let's take it to God. He can help her."

"You're right." He would pray diligently for Kylee to see her worth in God's eyes and in his, and maybe heaven could also nudge the incredible woman to give Chandler a chance.

His mom gave him a hug and said, "See you downstairs."

Chandler used the bathroom, brushed his teeth, and splashed on some cologne. He headed down the stairs to find most of the family assembled outside on Papa's back patio overlooking the lake. It was chilly even in early September in the mountains with the sun already down at seven, but it would've been too crowded inside, even though each of their houses were spacious.

A cheer went up. "Chandler!"

Family members surged toward him. Besides his cousin Maddie being off on some assignment, only his brother Greer, his cousin Alivia, and her fiancé Klein were gone. They were on guard duty until Thor, Esther, and her boyfriend Sheriff Reed went to relieve them after they ate dinner and had their meeting. Greer's new wife Emery was there too. They'd eloped shortly after Thor and Shelly's wedding. Nobody was surprised Greer opted for no fuss with his wedding, though their mom had been a little disappointed.

Emery was adorable and happy as ever. Chandler got hugs from everyone and was thrilled to see them all but itching to get to Kylee's side. She was seated at the outside dining table with a full plate in front of her, talking to Shelly and Melene.

Apparently he'd missed the prayer as everyone was either already eating or busy assembling their hamburgers and piling salads and side dishes on their plates. His family knew how to cook and enjoy delicious food.

Chandler took a plate and a long hug from Aunt Holly,

laughing at her comment of, "Wow, you just get more handsome every time I see you."

If only Kylee agreed.

"And you get more beautiful," he told his aunt.

"Oh, go on, you." She pushed a hand at him but beamed all the same.

He hurried to get salad, salsa, and chips and pile toppings on his hamburger bun, then went to see Papa at the grill for a double cheeseburger, bacon, and grilled onions. "Thanks, Papa."

"Of course." Papa stopped him with a hand on his arm and a serious look. "I have an idea of what exactly needs to happen, but ... I'm not sure about Kylee being involved."

Chandler's stomach turned over. That meant they were considering sending Kylee into extreme danger. He suddenly wasn't as hungry as he'd thought.

"It will have to be her choice," Papa said, his blue eyes somber.

"She's too brave to tell you no." Chandler wanted her to say no to whatever they were scheming.

"We'll see. She's the only clear option we can see." He was obviously struggling with his idea but knew it needed to happen.

Papa turned back to flipping hamburgers and Chandler wandered past. His neck prickled and his insides felt tied in knots. He didn't want Kylee anywhere close to danger. Yet if she could prevent nuclear winter and World War III, how could he selfishly keep her sheltered in his arms?

He walked up to where she was sitting on the end of a patio table. She smiled up at him, but it seemed guarded. Was she remembering how she'd pulled away from their almost-kiss? Did she even want to be in his arms?

Melene was seated between Kylee and Aiden. She pushed at Aiden. "Scoot down so Chandler can fit."

"He can sit on the ground," Aiden groused, but he moved for his girlfriend. Chandler didn't know that any of his brothers could tell their better halves no.

"Thank you, Melene." Chandler slid in next to Kylee. They were pressed tight. He liked it. Her arm and leg pressed against his while he tried to eat the messy hamburger and tease with his siblings and laugh at Shelly's funny quips. Kylee was wearing a long, fitted knit dress that hugged her curves. His mom had done well finding her clothes.

The happy atmosphere and Kylee's warmth and appeal almost made him forget about the danger that was pressing in on their family, the secret, and most especially on Kylee. Why did she have to be related to that awful Olivet Seamons? Why was she the only option Papa could see? Any of the well-trained Delta family members would happily go into danger, especially if it kept Kylee safe and stopped Frederick.

Kylee didn't say much during the meal, mostly observed and laughed. She didn't seem detached, but he could sense the huge family and his loud, obnoxious brothers overwhelmed her a little. Her grandpa and grandma were her only family, and they'd betrayed her. He knew she had no siblings, but did she not have any cousins either? That would be rough.

He looked around at his family. They were loud, intense, and sometimes too much but they were also loyal, fun, talented, hard-working, and he loved each of them deeply. His only regret playing professional lacrosse was missing out on times like these. Not being here enough for the people he loved.

As if Kylee sensed his gaze, she leaned closer to him and said, "You're very lucky. Your family is the best."

He looked down at her. As always, her dark eyes captivated him. "They are," he agreed. "You know who else is the best?"

She smiled sweetly up at him and his heart rate picked up. Maybe he did have a chance with her. "Who's that?"

"Thor!" Thor called from across the table. "The leader of the universe. That's who's the best." He stood and punched a fist in the air, then brought it to his chest.

Chandler shook his head. Leave it to his annoying brother to interrupt their moment.

Thor winked at him. "Sorry, bro. When you set me up for a slam dunk, I have to swing at it."

"Mixed metaphor," Kylee said, and everyone laughed.

"That's right, swing and an air ball," Shelly teased, though her green eyes were far too love-struck as she focused on her husband. "Leave those two alone. Pretend you're a newlywed and focus on your bride for a minute."

"Oh, I'll focus on my bride, and for a lot longer than a minute." Thor's eyes lit up and he sat back down, slid Shelly off her seat and onto his lap, and kissed her.

Melene and Aiden both laughed at the interaction. Chandler rolled his eyes, turning to look at Kylee. She was watching Thor and Shelly with a wistful expression. She glanced up at Chandler and the world disappeared. He wasn't a newlywed, but he could focus on his ... Kylee wasn't his anything, no matter how he wanted her to be.

"We need to meet downstairs before Thor, Esther, and Reed

go trade out Alivia, Klein, and Greer," Papa spoke from the next table over as everyone was finished eating.

"I know," Thor called, interrupting his kissing. "You need my expert opinion to save the world. Don't worry. I can take care of it single-handedly. That's what superheroes do."

"You're obnoxious, love," Shelly said.

"You love it."

"I love you."

He kissed her again.

"He's gotten more irritating and cocky over the years," Chandler whispered to Kylee. "If Hudson ever came home, he'd resume that role. But Thor decided he had to step in for now."

Kylee smiled at him. "I always liked Hudson."

"Great guy," Chandler agreed. Except for the brief visit for Thor's wedding, none of them but his parents had seen much of his little brother in years. Unless they opened TikTok, YouTube, or Instagram. They could see plenty of Hudson's insane stunts on those sites. The kid was a natural athlete and show-off, but they all worried he'd kill himself young. With the danger they were all facing, maybe Hudson was the smart one. Mama claimed he was hiding from his destiny. Whatever that meant.

"Thor and Shelly, keep on doing ... whatever it is you call that," Papa said good-naturedly. "Can everyone else please help clean up and convene in the conference room?"

Most of them laughed, but Aiden said loudly, "Melene, let's start making out and embarrass everyone around us. It'll be lots of fun and get us out of cleaning up dinner."

Chandler would happily clean up dinner if he could just get

one kiss from Kylee. His brothers were lucky men, and they knew it.

Shelly had already pulled away from Thor's lips at Papa's words. Now she glared at Aiden. "I know you're jealous."

Aiden gave her a strange look and drank a gulp of his water rather than responding to the weird jealous comment. Aiden had his own gorgeous girlfriend. Why would he be jealous of Thor kissing Shelly?

Kylee raised an eyebrow at Chandler. He shrugged, not sure what Shelly was trying to say.

The area quieted as everyone tried to figure out what Shelly meant by the comment. She and Aiden had never dated ... right?

Aiden downed more water as the moment became even more awkward.

"Everybody wishes they could be the one kissing Thor," Shelly said, all sugar and spice.

Aiden choked on his water and spit it across the table. It hit Thor and Shelly. They both jumped in surprise and everyone else laughed uproariously. The timing was perfect. Aiden should've felt justified, but he was still spluttering. "Kiss Thor ... oh, gross. Somebody get me a bowl. I am going to spew."

"Well, don't spew on us like you just spit on us," Thor called to him, escorting Shelly toward the serving table and grabbing a stack of napkins.

"Stop making out in front of all of us, or I'll spit on you some more," Aiden jabbed back.

Aiden took Melene's arm and they followed Thor and Shelly into the house, still verbally sparring while Thor and Shelly blotted the wetness off.

Chandler looked at Kylee. "Sorry." He shrugged. "My family. They're a little crazy at times." Crazy was putting it mildly as he tried to survey all the teasing from an outside perspective.

"No, don't apologize." She gestured around the patio at various family members still laughing about Aiden spitting on Thor as they stacked food to carry it inside. "You're very lucky to be part of a family like this."

Chandler knew he was, even if they did get out of control sometimes. He hated that she didn't have love, trust, and safety of a strong family. How did he offer to make her part of his family? They'd all welcome her with opens arms, but she'd probably scoff at him even thinking that. She assumed he was a player who'd never settle down. What would she say if he told her she'd always been his dream woman and he'd settle down with her in an instant? Would she kiss him like she had as a teenager? Then how long would it take before she sent him a text and broke his heart? No, he couldn't think like that. They'd been young, and he had to forgive and move past that, but sadly she didn't seem to want to give him a chance again and move past his womanizer reputation.

Kylee started stacking the paper plates that his brothers and their ladies had left behind in their argument. They'd all be humiliated if they knew she was cleaning up after them. He helped her and they carried piles to the garbage.

The cleanup went quickly and before he knew it, Chandler was walking through Papa's house next to Kylee, headed for the basement and the conference room. It suddenly felt like they were walking to their doomsday. He could almost hear the music cueing some creepy tune. If only he could sweep her away from all of this. She was safer here with his family than anywhere on the planet. Until they asked her to go risk her life. At least they knew if they could keep Frederick from obtaining the secret, he wouldn't launch his nukes. Even that insane masochist didn't want to risk destroying the fabled "Delta weapon."

Chandler wasn't one to question authority. He'd been respectful of his parents, grandparents, coaches, teachers, and church leaders all his life. At the moment, he felt a desperate need to first tell Papa that Kylee would not be involved in any crazy scheme to take down Frederick. Chandler would spirit her away to a Caribbean island that nobody cared to bomb and protect her there.

Second, he wanted to know what the secret was. He and his siblings and cousins teased and discussed, and no subject was taboo ... except the secret and the secret keeper. Occasionally he'd had a private conversation speculating with one of them but mostly they all knew to their core that if they couldn't trust Papa, the world might as well end. So when their beloved Papa said he couldn't reveal the secret, none of them had questioned that. To his knowledge. Now Chandler felt driven to know and understand what they were sacrificing so much for. What was so important that a dangerous dictator would hold off on his plans of world domination to obtain it? His family had all promised to protect this secret, and they didn't even know what it was.

"You okay?" Kylee looked up at him as they reached the bottom of the basement steps.

"Not really," he admitted.

"I can feel the stress radiating off you."

He stopped and looked down at her. "And to think yesterday

morning my biggest stress was if we'd go into the playoffs with a win."

She studied him. "I'm sorry I brought this on you. On your family."

"Oh, Kylee, no." Chandler shook his head. "If you hadn't brought your message, we'd all be in infinitely more danger. I just want to keep you safe." He couldn't resist gathering her close and hugging her.

Kylee melted against him. "Thank you, Chandler. I feel safe with you." She looked up, her dark gaze full of him.

Without her heels on, she didn't reach his shoulder. He could easily remedy that. He lifted her off her feet and bowed his head to kiss her.

"Sheesh! Not you two as well. Do any of my brothers know the meaning of making out in private?" Aiden's voice was far too close.

Chandler lowered Kylee's feet to the ground and released her, turning to glare at his brother and Melene. Sadly, it was impossible to glare at Melene. She was so altruistic and charitable you'd have to be a devil to not react positively to her sweetness.

"Ooh, the look. He's giving us the look." Aiden walked past, holding Melene's hand.

Chandler barely restrained himself from punching him. "Sorry," he muttered to Kylee.

She looked unsteady and confused. "It's okay. I probably shouldn't anyway." She bit at her lip and he was the one confused now.

"Shouldn't?" Shouldn't kiss him? Why in the heck not? They really needed to have a thorough chat about how he was not a player, and if she hadn't written him off at sixteen, they'd probably have one of those long distance high school sweetheart straight to marriage kind of stories.

Uncle Joseph and Aunt Holly walked past, giving them kind smiles but saying nothing.

He looked back up the stairs, but it was quiet. A loud rumble was coming from the conference room. They were probably the only ones left out here.

"We'd better get in there," Kylee said, as if noticing the same thing.

"Kylee." Chandler moved quickly and pinned her against the wall. Her eyes widened and her mouth looked soft and kissable. He wanted to kiss her but keeping her safe, and hopefully someday gaining her trust, was infinitely more important. "This meeting is going to be hard, but I am going to be there for you, no matter what."

She blinked up at him. "Thank you, Chandler."

"And after all this settles, I want to spend more time with you. I want to date you. I want to show you I'm not a player."

She blinked up at him and he wasn't sure if she believed him. He wanted to groan in frustration, but he held her gaze, willing her to know he was sincere. She was the right woman for him. He'd known it as a sixteen-year-old, and being around her again had only solidified it.

"Chandler? Kylee?" Papa's voice was soft, but he was obviously waiting for them.

"Coming." Chandler kept his gaze on her. He was out of time to convince her to date him, but he had to tell her right now. "And please remember you can tell Papa no. You do what is right for you, not for the Delta secret."

She licked her lips and nodded. He could feel her trembling. He didn't blame her for being nervous. He was terrified about countless things. What was going to happen with the nightmare Frederick was creating was high on the list, but above it was whether he could ever convince Kylee to trust and love him.

Chapter Ten

Chandler took Kylee's hand and led her into his family meeting. She couldn't stop trembling. Chandler probably thought it was because she was scared of what was to come, but the real reason was how he affected her. She still loved him, just as she had as a silly teenager. It was even stronger now and she would be stupider than her teenage self to fall for him again, especially as the world might end tomorrow.

Yet if the world ended tomorrow, why wouldn't she take a few delicious kisses from Chandler to take with her on her walk to the pearly gates? Could she and Chandler develop a relationship in the next life? Without social media, lacrosse, Delta secrets, evil dictators, and all the women throwing themselves at him? What a weird question to have at this moment.

They entered the large conference room. She counted twenty-four chairs and more than half of them filled. Every eye seemed to be on her and Chandler. She'd brought the information to them and these people were highly trained and experienced, but somehow she knew it would fall on her to help end Frederick.

You're pathetic. A teacher from inner-city Chicago taking on King Frederick?

Sadly, Mimi was right this time, and Kylee didn't even try to tell her to be quiet. This was insane. She glanced at Greer's wife Emery. She was a teacher as well, and already heavily involved in the secret her brother had died for. Emery's brother had died on the opposite side of the Deltas, trying to steal the secret from them. Just like her grandma and grandpa were trying to help King Frederick do. There was a strange comfort in that. The Deltas didn't judge Emery for her brother doing evil deeds, and they didn't seem to judge Kylee for her rotten family either.

Chandler escorted her to a chair, helped her settle into it, sat at her side, and then reached for her hand again. She felt like they were a couple, just like most of the others in the room were. A few eyebrows raised as she clasped his hand tightly. She shouldn't let him or his family think they were dating, but she really needed the support and strength of her lacrosse superstar right now. Her *el campeón.*

"Thanks everybody for getting here. I'll try to make this brief so we can rotate out guard duty and those who have the second night shift or early morning duty can get some sleep. I'll brief Alivia, Klein, and Greer when they return."

A few nods, but most just sat tensely in their chairs. Kylee felt her own stress level rising at the intense look in each of the Delta family's blue eyes. It was an odd thing to think about at the moment, but in most of the world, brown was the predominant eye color. Not tonight. Myrna and Shelly both had green eyes, and

Emery, Melene, and Reed had dark-brown like her. The rest were piercing blue, like Chandler's.

Cue the infatuated sigh.

Por favor quedate quieto. She'd added please because she really did need to calm down around this irresistible man.

"Everyone has been briefed on the message Kylee overheard and is up to date on the escalated threat from Frederick?" Papa looked around the table and received a lot more nods.

Kylee was impressed how much they all trusted Papa Delta—and her. Her grandparents were part of the reason for the nightmare coming at the Delta family and their country if Frederick succeeded. Yet Papa and these people trusted what she'd overheard and were willing to fight to protect the secret and their country.

"So we must assume that Ross, or Olivet, was the one who revealed the secret to King Frederick. They are traitors to our country." He gave Kylee a sympathetic look. She held his gaze, willing him to know she would be all right, as long as Chandler kept holding her hand. She kept telling herself not to fall for him, but she needed him—his support, his strength, his ability to comfort and protect her.

"Papa," Chandler interrupted him. "Does Admiral Seamons know what the secret is?"

Papa shook his head. "Admiral Seamons doesn't know. He only knows about it because, Josh, one of the creators, told him he was working on something huge and Ross came to me about it. I never told him what it was capable of. Nobody but myself, the creators, and the person I appoint as secret keeper will ever know what the secret is. Unless the worst happens," he said in an undertone.

"Frederick thinks it's a weapon that will make him the most powerful man on earth." Chandler looked to Kylee. She nodded. He seemed nervous to keep going and no one else said a word. They seemed to be holding their breath and waiting for something to happen.

Chandler locked gazes with his grandfather. "Is it a weapon?"

The tension ramped up. She waited in suspense along with everyone else as the seconds ticked by and Papa simply stared at Chandler. She could easily read that they all wanted to know and maybe had been waiting for this moment for a long time but their respect for Papa had held them in check. She thought Chandler deeply respected his grandfather but it felt like it was past time the entire family had some answers.

Papa looked away from Chandler and his gaze focused on the youngest Delta, Jessica. Kylee remembered how adorable and well-loved Jessie had been when she'd first visited the family. She still seemed like a sweetheart, but she was much quieter than Kylee remembered.

Colton, Chandler's oldest cousin, cleared his throat and drew everyone's attention. Kylee wondered if she should excuse herself. These people had earned the right to know what the secret was by their devotion to their family and to the secret's protection. What had she done? Yet if she was going to be asked by Papa to confront Mimi and possibly King Frederick, she was in as deep as anybody.

"Papa," Colton began in a gravelly tone. "You know we're all willing to fight and die for you and the secret, just as we've always been."

Several family members nodded.

"We've all tried not to ask out of respect for you, and like you've always taught us, to keep us and secret safe."

Kylee wondered if Colton was trying to tell Chandler he shouldn't have asked the question. He surprised her when he continued, "But we're all adults now and I would trust anyone in this room with any secret and with my own life." Colton looked around the room and Kylee felt honored to be here. Did he really mean that? She didn't know Colt very well, but he was more serious than the rest of the family and it was easy to trust him and look up to him like an older, trustworthy brother.

"You understand I've been trying to protect all of you as much as the secret," Papa said quietly.

Kylee could hardly imagine the heavy burden Papa carried. To protect some huge secret, have his entire family involved, and want to keep all those he loved safe as well as protect America.

"We do," Colton continued. "We respect and love you, Papa."

Most of the heads bobbed in agreement, but even Colton's parents and Chandler's parents seemed content to let Colton lead the way on this.

"Can we at least know ..." Colton paused as if trying to figure out how to phrase the question to get some information without being disrespectful, putting any of them needlessly in danger, or pushing Papa too hard. "Is it a weapon, and if not, why do all the rumors point that direction?"

Papa looked at him for a few beats. Kylee could almost feel everyone in the room hold their breath. Chandler's hand tightened around hers. This family was crazy loyal to each other and to Papa Delta. To think they'd all committed to protect some secret and they had no idea if it was a cure to toe fungus or a bio-chemical weapon. It was singularly impressive to her.

"I know all the secrecy isn't easy," Papa began, "Especially as you all have proven your loyalty and devotion to your family and to the secret." He paused. Kylee could almost sense the room's disappointment, but still no one demanded to know. Papa looked up at the ceiling and then back at Colton. "It is a highly-specialized weapon. The likes of which the world has never seen."

Everyone pulled in a collective breath. In any other setting, after such a proclamation Kylee would think there would be murmuring, questions, maybe a few curse words.

"That is all I feel I can tell you, for your own safety as well as the secret's. Do you understand?" Papa was more intense than Kylee had imagined he could ever get. But this was an intense moment.

She was stunned once again how fully these people trusted her. She could easily be a plant from her evil grandmother and be transmitting any information back to Chicago and on to King Frederick. Not one of the family looked at her as if they suspected she would ever do something so underhanded. If Papa and Chandler trusted her, they did as well. She loved these people. If only she could be part of this family. She glanced quickly at Chandler. He met her gaze and she had to look away before she begged him to never let her go.

"Thank you, Papa," Myrna said. "For sharing that. I know the level of trust you have in each of us to reveal that much."

Papa gave a half smile. "I'd trust any of you with my life." He looked slowly around the room. "But the Delta secret is much, much more important than my life."

Some of the family protested at that. Papa held up a hand. "I'm an old used-up man missing the love of my life." He smiled wryly at them, then got serious again. "But I want you all to know that each of you is more important to me than any secret, any weapon, anything on earth."

"Thank you, Papa," Jessie said softly.

Kylee felt the sting of tears being included in such a proclamation. For some crazy reason, she felt like Papa valued her as much as anyone else in the room. But he couldn't. Not like his own children, grandchildren, or those marrying into the family. Could he?

There was also the sting—no, it was a gouged-out wound—of her grandparents not caring about her at all. Instead of showing their granddaughter, their only descendant, that she was important to them, they'd sent a hitman after her simply because they thought she'd overheard Mimi's evil plans. She shivered. Chandler rubbed his thumb along the back of her hand and sent tingles up her arm. She glanced at him and the look in his blue eyes was sincere, warm, and committed. To her.

Was he for real? Could she hope he wouldn't bail on her after enjoying a few days or a week together? Would he break her heart again like he had at sixteen, or were they both more mature and ready for a relationship? What about all those women he'd dated or was currently dating? He was probably missing dates to be here, just like he was missing practice. Once this all settled, he'd surely want to go back to his busy, fun, rewarding, and women-filled life.

She shook away those thoughts as Papa moved on. "We've been using all the communication we are privy to and the connections we trust and we found the *innocent* businessman, at least a businessman who hasn't been caught for his fraud and murders yet, that King Frederick will use to fly into Chicago Saturday night."

Kylee's eyes widened and horror made her stomach pitch. She could see similar expressions throughout the room. She thought it, but Esther was the one who said, "But Papa, that's in two days."

"Yes, love," Papa said.

"How are we going to get set up to protect Kylee at that party in less than forty-eight hours?" Esther's voice sounded desperate.

All eyes turned to Kylee, and she wished she hadn't enjoyed all of that delicious food as she was tasting it again. Her worst fears were about to come true. They were going to ask her to walk into a party with Mimi and King Frederick. What did they think she could accomplish? Her grandmother and Frederick might torture and kill her simply for the sport of it.

"She's not going into some party with the woman who sent a hitman after her, and King Frederick as well," Chandler protested for her. "Frederick's a psychotic masochist."

Kylee could add that her grandmother was just as bad, but at least her grandmother wasn't murdering people in mass amounts, maybe just in singles.

"I know, son, and I told you it would be her choice." Papa looked back at her. "Kylee ... we need you to walk into that party and get close enough to Frederick to get a hair sample from him."

"A hair sample?" Aiden clarified.

Papa nodded and looked back at her. "Then you can get out of there. We're going to find a way to get Bailey, Klein, and Reed in as servers." Bailey gave her a brave smile while Chandler held on tighter to her hand. The sheriff nodded to Kylee from his spot next to Esther. She knew Klein was the well-built contractor guy marrying Alivia, but he was on guard duty right now. "You'll all have cameras on so we can get proof of who attends the party, helping us get a better bead on who's loyal to our country or not."

"Smart," Aiden said. "I'll happily interrogate any of them."

Papa smiled but didn't comment.

"Bailey is going to try to get the hair as well, but as a server she might not get close enough. He's all about class distinctions." Papa's voice was full of disgust. "But Frederick also loves beautiful women, so we're hoping one of you can get close enough to use the small kit you'll have with you, a small tool that will quickly rip out some of his hairs and the follicles as well, then you'll slip it into the container and give the word. Bailey, Klein, and Reed will surround you and get you safely out of the house, where we'll be waiting."

Kylee's heart was beating high and fast at the idea of waltzing into that party and getting intimately close to one of the most dangerous men in the world. Would Mimi shoot her on sight?

"The rest of us are too recognizable to get in and out undetected, and we have no way to alter the guest list."

"I'm not on that list," Kylee said.

"No, but it is at your grandparent's home, so we're hoping you can bluff your way in."

She probably could. The staff they usually hired all knew and liked her. She wondered if Papa Delta really could trade out servers. Mimi was very particular about who she let in her home and Kylee knew most of them by sight if not name.

"We will be outside, and if things go badly, we'll hang the consequences and crash the party. I've let slip to the government officials I trust that Frederick is making a trip to our soil. It's bold of him, but so far I'm getting the 'red tape' and 'we're not involved in the conflict yet and can't risk an incident' jabber." He shook his head. "Heaven willing, we can get some kind of solid proof to have your grandparents arrested and Frederick caught and removed from power, but I'm not counting on it. Unfortunately, even my contacts who trust me aren't willing to risk an international confrontation based on a conversation overheard from a pantry."

Kylee felt the sting of that, but she'd known it would be that way. The fact that all these people trusted her meant the world to her.

"A hair?" she managed to ask. What could a hair do?

Papa simply smiled and splayed his hands. "It will be useful soon."

The family members looked at each other or shifted in their chairs, but nobody questioned Papa.

"I don't want her doing this," Chandler protested again.

"I understand," Papa said kindly. He looked to Kylee. "It's up to you. Nobody will blame you if you say no."

Kylee looked around the room. They were all impressive and qualified. They'd trusted her with secrets, included her in their family circle, and they needed her. She wanted to help; she had to at least try, especially because her grandparents were responsible for this mess.

"I'll do it."

Chandler's jaw tightened and so did his grip on her hand. He studied her, begging her to change her mind, but she could see that he would let her choose.

"A tailor will come tomorrow," Papa interrupted her from staring at Chandler, "and fit Kylee for formal wear. I will teach you how to use your mic, earpiece, and camera, and how to extract the hair most effectively. Chandler will teach you some effective self-defense moves in case Frederick or anyone else tries to restrain you. I apologize that you or Bailey will have to flirt with and get close enough to Frederick to retrieve the hair."

Kylee shuddered, but shrugged. She met Bailey's gaze and could see the lady was nervous as well, but Bailey said confidently, "It's okay. I already knew self-defense before I met Colt and I figure if I can take my tough boyfriend down, King Frederick is no match for me."

Everyone laughed at that. All these men were unreal tough, but Colton was the oldest cousin, more serious than most, and probably had combat training military special ops teams would envy.

Colt grinned and gestured to Bailey. "She's telling the truth. Took me down when I tried to kiss her the first time."

"I know how to stop the handsy ones," Bailey said.

They all laughed louder, and it looked like Colt was actually blushing. Kylee really appreciated the break in tension.

Papa stood as the laughter settled. "I'll have assignments for those who are going by the morning. We will leave for the airport Saturday at eight a.m. Thank you all." His gaze focused on Bailey and Kylee. "Especially both of you."

Others in the room seconded Papa's thanks. Kylee's cheeks burned, and she tried to smile and show that she was accepting their gratitude, but it was pretty overwhelming. No one but her could waltz into that party like they belonged. Sadly, she was the least qualified of the group for special ops and she had no idea if her grandmother would pretend all was well for the sake of the party or order her killed for the party's entertainment. Could Bailey, Reed, and Klein really spirit her out of there, or would Mimi's men intercept them?

Thor, Esther, and Reed took off first, and then the rest of the group slowly dispersed.

Colt and Bailey made their way over to them. Bailey held out her hand. "Chicago chicks unite."

Kylee smiled and took her hand.

Bailey squeezed it tight. "We're going to rock this mission. Klein and Reed are super tough and will watch out for us. But I have to tell you, my friend, I really can kick any man's butt, so if you have any trouble you just say into the earpiece and I'm there. Nobody will suspect a thing." She released Kylee's hand and gestured to herself. "They get distracted by the pretty face and before they know it, they've lost an eye."

Kylee reared back. "That escalated quickly."

Bailey smiled, looking innocent and beautiful. Was she really some tough and confident weapon? "If some idiot is going to hurt you, I'll take him out any way I see fit. Then I'll write a disparaging story about them. This is great research, actually." She winked, then sobered. "Seriously, friend. I'm so impressed with your bravery and we will keep you safe." She gave her an impulsive hug, and then she and Colt walked away.

Kylee drew in a breath and looked at Chandler.

"You all right?" he asked.

"Hmm." She shrugged.

"This is too much to ask of you. I'll tell Papa to come up with a new plan." His jaw was tight and his blue eyes determined.

"No, Chandler." Kylee shook her head. "I have to do this."

He studied her, and something in her eyes must've convinced him as he finally nodded, looking miserable but resigned. He would stand up for her, but she had to do this.

"My grandparents are straight-up evil," she continued, "and your family not only trusts me but is protecting me, and the world, and some secret weapon. All you're asking of me is to flirt with some loser and steal his hair." She tried for brave, but her voice was shaky. "I can do this."

He looked over her and said, "You are extremely brave like Bailey said. I'm so impressed with you, Kylee."

"Thank you," she managed, going under the power of those blue eyes again and forgetting about everything else.

"Chandler, Kylee." Papa walked up to them, and Kylee realized they were the only ones left in the room. His blue eyes focused in on Kylee and though they were crystal clear and bright like Chandler's, they had a very different power. "I can't imagine how overwhelming this is. Thank you for your willingness to help."

She shook her head. "Papa, thank you." She swallowed and continued on, "You believe me, you've all protected me, fed me, clothed me."

Ohana means family, she thought of the line from Lilo and Stitch. *Family means nobody gets left behind.* Her own family didn't watch out for her, but the Deltas would.

She blinked to clear the emotion and almost admitted how terribly alone she was, but instead she forced a watery smile. "I love your family. Always have." She didn't let herself look at Chandler, but she could feel the intensity of his stare. "Even though it's under hard circumstances, I'm very, very grateful to be here with you and very, very grateful for you and your expertise and kick-buttedness."

Papa smiled at her last word, but then he reached out and gathered her close. Something about his build and even his smell —was it seriously Old Spice?—reminded her of her grandpa and the tears she'd been fighting threatened to spill over. She hugged him back and then pulled away.

Papa looked very serious as he said, "You always have a spot here with us, Kylee. Always."

"Thanks," she managed.

"And just between the two of us ..." He lowered his voice and looked out the open conference room door. "I keep praying that Ross is innocent. I just can't believe that loyal, brave, good-to-the-bone man could betray his country, but more especially that he could ever let harm come to you. The military is good at building hard shells around lifelong soldiers. Ross doesn't know how to show his affection, but he loves you, Kylee, and he wouldn't let anybody hurt you."

The tears spilled over then. She wanted to believe him, but were they both deluded? She reached for the necklace that wasn't there. Her grandfather had given her that necklace. He had tried to shelter her from Mimi's barbs but had mostly failed. How could he be married to Mimi for all these years and not have her evil rub off on him?

Papa smiled and then turned and walked away. Chandler said nothing, as if letting her soak in the words.

She blew out a breath and turned to him. "Shall we start on self-defense training tonight?"

He looked her over as if she were fragile emotionally. "We can wait until the morning."

"No." She shook her head. "I need to be ready to walk into that party with confidence."

You, confident? That's a laugh.

Spegnerlo!

She swallowed hard. There was no world where she could walk into that party with true confidence, but at least she could feel better knowing she could defend herself. If only she could undo all the negative Mimi had put into her head.

Chandler's gaze was warm on her. "You can, Kylee. You can hold your head high knowing the Delta family has your back and God will be watching over you as well."

She liked that a lot. She would pray harder than ever and hopefully the Deltas and heaven would carry her through with minimal injury, physical or emotional.

"Plus..." He eased in closer. "You'll easily be the most gorgeous woman at that party. Distracting King Frederick and everyone else with your beauty."

Her eyes widened.

Gorgeous? Beauty? Ha! You? Tell the boy he is delus—

"I know you try to dismiss every compliment given to you," he said huskily, his blue eyes full of meaning and his sincere words miraculously cutting off Mimi's voice. "But believe me, Kylee. You are the most beautiful woman I have ever seen in my life. Beauty that starts inside and radiates out. You shine with pure, innocent, irresistible beauty."

Kylee blinked at him. Were his words as genuine and heartfelt as they seemed? His gaze said they were. His blue eyes were begging her to believe him. It was the most touching and sincere compliment she'd ever received. She wanted to internalize it. She wanted to kiss him, but she needed time to process his words. She'd had a pastor once tell her she was enough to her Father in Heaven and if she could truly believe that, she would never doubt her eternal worth again. Chandler's sincere gaze and compliment seemed to back up that pastor's words. God loved her and saw her worth, and Chandler seconded it. What more did she need?

Chapter Eleven

Kylee stepped back away from Chandler, needing time to process and dissect his profound words, and how he'd managed to shut down Mimi's snark mid-sentence. The other option was throwing herself into his arms and begging him to kiss her.

The emotions fighting inside her were getting far too intense. She needed to focus on this terrifying party first, and then maybe she could try to internalize what Chandler was saying and sort out if they could truly have a future.

"Where should we do the training?" she asked.

He looked surprised and Kylee almost laughed, despite how serious everything felt. Had he ever had a woman not fall to his feet? Was he really some womanizer? She'd assumed so and wasn't sure she wanted the full story.

"There's an empty bedroom just down the hall," he said.

"Perfect." She walked out into the hallway, and he stepped up to her side and directed her to an open door. The room was carpeted and had a window with a concrete window well and a closet, but nothing else.

Chandler stepped up close and gave her an appealing smile. "Don't worry. I'll be gentle with you."

"Do I look that nervous?" she asked.

He shrugged, not refuting or denying.

Folding her arms across her chest, Kylee tried for sassy. "I'm not some wussy girl. By the end of tonight, I'll take you down and have you begging for mercy."

A slow smile grew on his face. He knew she was bluffing, but he liked her words. "Sounds good, beautiful. I'd love to have you 'take me down.'"

Kylee's breath came quicker and the thought of somehow knocking him to the floor, then pinning him down and kissing him made her hot all over.

He edged in closer. "I can't wait to be begging for mercy after you take me down." His gaze trailed slowly over her, those irresistible eyes having the power to take her under. "I'll be begging for mercy for my heart, that's for sure. Because you've completely captured it." His voice was husky and so irresistible.

Kylee blinked in surprise. Could he mean that? It was one thing for the ultimate player to tease and get every girl to kiss him, but would he really claim she'd captured his heart? It couldn't be true. He couldn't mean it deeply, not like she felt it. He was a natural flirt. End of story. *La fin.*

"Let's focus on the self-defense," she all but begged.

He studied her, but something in her demeanor must've convinced him to slow down on all the tender and beautiful declarations that she couldn't fully process or internalize right now.

He cleared his throat and immediately got serious. "Okay. You're going to be a lot smaller than your opponent, so you'll have to fight dirty."

"Unlike you with your big muscles and superior training." He didn't mean smaller—he meant weaker. Right? She'd never be defined as "small."

"Hey, glad you call it like it is." He sobered quickly. "Seriously, Kylee. I've been trained to fight since I was a child, and you can bet King Frederick and his bodyguards will have expert training as well. The sheer strength of a man is always going to be more than yours, even if he's close to your same size."

"Hey, I'm tough." She folded her arms defiantly across her chest. She did Pilates, yoga, strength training, and walked. She wasn't muscle-bound tough like King Frederick's bodyguards probably would be. She hadn't even thought about bodyguards; she had only worried about Mimi's security guys.

"Even if he's close to your same size," ran through her mind.

That was telling. He was admitting she was short but not small.

Chandler's eyes traveled over her like a warm caress. "You have a beautiful shape and it's obvious you exercise and are strong," he said.

Kylee backed up instinctively. He couldn't mean that. She tried to be fit, but her body was smooth and rounded. She'd never been able to develop showy muscles, even when she'd gone to the gym faithfully for over two years and lifted heavy weights four to five days a week in addition to intense cardio.

"My sister and female cousins have the training to take down any man," Chandler continued, "but they have to use

126

different strategies and tactics. Men are naturally physically stronger. It's the way the Lord built us so we could protect our women."

She nodded, willing to accept it because there wasn't any way to change the way men and women were physically built. The way he'd put it was a bit less acceptable. *Protect our women?* Was she just one of Chandler's women? The thought churned her stomach but miraculously Mimi's cutting words didn't play through her mind. Had Chandler somehow ousted the nagging?

"So if someone is coming after you or has you in his grip, use anything you can think of to get free and cause damage."

She drew in a breath and tried to look unafraid.

"Papa will have a knife sewn into your dress and tomorrow we'll train on how to rip the seam and access it."

Her eyes widened.

"It'll be hard to think straight when you're scared, but focus on vulnerable spots—the eyes, mouth, neck, groin. You've probably heard about people stomping on somebody's instep, and that's another good one. Especially with those high heels you like to wear." He grinned as if her heels were irresistible. "If you can't get to the knife, any kind of weapon you can see will be helpful—car keys, a kitchen knife, a tool, anything in your reach. Poke them in a sensitive spot and you should be able to get an opening to run. Bailey, Reed, and Klein will be in the house and the rest of us will be there quick if you're in danger."

It all sounded absolutely horrible. Grab a knife and poke someone in the eye?

"You look so innocent and scared." His entire body softened, and he passed a hand over his face. "Are you sure you can do this?

Papa can figure out a way to come up with another plan or Bailey can just go in."

"It needs to be me," she insisted, and she felt the truth of her words all way through. She was the only one who could waltz into that party like she owned the place and somehow she'd pray hard enough to have the confidence to get the hair from King Frederick but also to stand up to her grandmother. She squared her shoulders. "I'm going to be fine, Chandler, and I still think I can take you down."

"You're incredible." His eyes filled with appreciation.

She wanted to hold on to this moment, but she needed to be ready for the party in less than forty-eight hours. "What should we work on first?"

His blue eyes were still warm, but he nodded. "Shall we practice you breaking a few holds? But maybe don't poke my eye out." He winked.

He wrapped his arms around her lower back and had her pinned tight against his chest before she realized what had happened. His breath seemed to come as quick as hers, and the way his breath brushed her cheek made her light-headed. He smelled clean and irresistibly fresh. If he moved his mouth just enough, their lips would brush. Her heart hammered in her ears.

"Okay, love." Chandler's words were a caress against her cheek. He hadn't called her a term of endearment since he first held her at the lacrosse game, and it made her weak for him. She leaned into his hold, which she was certain was the exact wrong move if he had been a bad guy.

"Don't really hurt me," he continued, though it didn't sound like he thought she could hurt him, "but if somebody has you face-to-face like this, a quick knee to the groin is always a good option, but you have to mean it and you have to do it quick."

Her eyes widened. She could not do that to him. He'd devastated her emotionally at sixteen, but she would never want to hurt him. What did she want? Mostly an apology and for him to convince her he'd never ditch her again.

He chuckled and released her. She staggered, unsteady by the sudden loss of his touch. "Bring your knee up quick and show me."

She tried to obey, but it was obviously lacking conviction and wouldn't be effective.

"Since the person would have you wrapped up, you can actually use that against him." He didn't comment on her pathetic attempt but rested his hands loosely on her shoulders. "Grab onto my biceps and use that to stabilize yourself as you bring your knee up hard."

She wrapped her hands around his biceps, but she couldn't focus. His muscles were perfectly developed and she really enjoyed touching them. It brought her back to that magical summer and how every touch had been full of tingles and promise. She hadn't believed in either for a long time, but with Chandler so close, the hope of a future with this incredible man was shimmering and maybe even within reach.

"Okay. Bring your knee up." He stayed a safe distance away, but she used his arms as a stabilizer and brought her knee up much harder and surer than before. She was proud of herself for reacting when her mind was completely distracted.

"Perfect," he said. "Now I release you for just a second, and what do you do?"

Get lost in his captivating blue eyes? No, that wasn't right. "R-Run?"

"Yes. If at all possible, get away, and with your earpiece in and the camera and mic on, we'll be coming for you as soon as you are in trouble. Bailey, Reed, and Klein will be moments away."

That was reassuring. "Thank you," she said.

He nodded, but before she could say anything else, his hands moved quickly and he flipped her around to face away from him, wrapping his arms tight around her abdomen. "Okay. Someone comes at you from behind. Any ideas?"

"Um ..." Enjoy the feel of his arms? Ask him how he developed such nice muscles in his chest? Was that all lacrosse, Delta training, or did he do weight training as well?

She could not think straight. She loved being close to him far too much. All the memories of him that she'd clung to, even as she tried to forget them, were intermingling with all the sweet, and she thought sincere, words he'd said earlier. She was filled with the desperate hope that Chandler could not just be in her future but *be* her future.

If she tilted her head back and kissed him, what would he do?

"The instep thing?" she fumbled to ask instead of giving into the desire filling her.

"Yes, perfect. Stomp down hard on his instep, elbow him down low, and then if that doesn't work, jab your elbow back into his neck. Try it out."

She went through the motions, not really hitting him.

Chandler gently turned her to face him but released her from his grasp. "Good. We'll keep working on a lot more tomorrow. Especially how to pull the knife out, once the tailor comes and we figure out where to sew it in. We can't prepare for everything, but the most important thing is to use your knife, or any weapon you can reach, and try to get away. A man will be strong, but everyone is vulnerable and like I said, we'll be coming for you, so don't stress." He stopped talking and studied her.

"Are you?" she asked, completely enraptured by his gaze.

He arched an eyebrow. "Am I ...?"

"Vulnerable." She loved the way his thick brown lashes outlined his blue eyes.

He swallowed, and then a soft smile crossed his face. It wasn't his usual smile; it was ... vulnerable. He didn't say anything, and the silence stretched to almost awkward. Kylee was tempted to back away and change the subject, but something was happening between them and her guard was down and she was more vulnerable than she wanted to admit. She wanted him and hoped she wouldn't live to regret it when he ghosted her and went back to his famous life and dating every other girl.

"Kylee." His voice was deep and unsteady. He took a deep breath and said, "There's always been something in your eyes that makes me feel like I'm a superstar. Like I'm the best man in the world."

She saw him as that, but it was interesting that he felt something so deep when she looked at him. She felt a similar way—his blue eyes swept her away, made her feel like the only woman he'd ever want or need, and made her forget the hurt falling for him could cause. The connection between them was pulsing, and she wanted to insulate the line and not let it fray. But it had frayed before, just like her only connection to her family had frayed. She was terrified of being hurt and alone again.

He stepped in closer. "But then I get scared to let you see how vulnerable I am to you." He reached up and gently framed her face with his palms. His right thumb gently caressed her lips, and she let out a soft sigh. He leaned in. "I'm scared to get hurt again."

That made her eyes widen. Him get hurt? She was the one who got hurt last time.

"The connection I felt to you when we were sixteen ... it's even stronger now. I've always felt like you were the only woman in the world for me."

Kylee was completely speechless. That was exactly how she'd felt and all she'd hoped for him to feel. But why had he never called or texted? She'd been too low in self-confidence to make the first move. Now she was confused, but his words also touched her deeply.

She should pull back and ask him why he hadn't called, ask him if he was a heartbreaking womanizer or if he could be true to her. She should demand to know the truth. No flirtations, no lines.

But for all her languages and linguistic skills, all she could do was stare at him.

Chandler's thumb traced her lips again, making her tremble. He gently slid his hands into her hair and caressed her scalp as he pulled her even closer. His breath warmed her lips and his strong body overshadowed her. She'd never felt a sensation so thrilling.

And then his lips met hers.

Fireworks seemed to explode within her, and she knew that thrilling wasn't strong enough. The kiss was a mind-blowing connection that marked her his and him hers. It was unreal. She'd only felt a connection like this when she'd kissed him for the first time at sixteen.

She instinctively wrapped her arms around him and tried to pull him closer. Chandler slid his hands down her back and molded their bodies together. She was full of heat and light and love. Chandler Delta was the man for her, and her lips and her body and her soul all agreed.

Much, much later, he pulled back from the kiss and tenderly kissed her cheek, her forehead, her hairline. "We'd better get some rest," he said softly.

Kylee wanted him to profess his love, but he had said earlier she was the only woman in the world for him. That was huge. If she could truly believe that, it could have the power to change her world.

"Okay," she managed.

He swept her off her feet and against his strong chest. Kylee cried out in surprise, wrapping her arms around his neck for stability. "Put me down. I'm too heavy," she protested.

Chandler's cheek crinkled in a grin. "Heavy?" He scoffed. "Kylee, you are not heavy." He carried her out of the room and easily ascended the first flight of steps to the foyer. The foyer light and outdoor lights were still on, but it was obvious Papa had gone to bed. Kylee wanted Chandler to convince her she wasn't heavy, that he really did think she was "perfect." It seemed like a cruel joke that he would say those things if he didn't mean them. Mimi would laugh, that was for sure.

Crazily enough, Kylee hadn't heard Mimi's mocking voice in her head since Chandler had interrupted it and said the beautiful words, *You are the most beautiful woman I have ever seen in my life. Beauty that starts inside and radiates out. You shine with pure, innocent, irresistible beauty.*

She loved those words and wanted to write them down, engrave them on a bracelet, repeat them every day. Suddenly she couldn't care less what Mimi thought. She was in Chandler's arms and not even her evil grandmother could touch her here.

Chandler carried her up the grand staircase to the second story without missing a step or even getting short of breath.

He stole a quick kiss, then lowered her to her feet. She pressed into him and she could feel his heart racing and his breath speeding up.

"Sorry, carrying me got you all out of breath," she said, looking up into his handsome face.

"What?" He laughed. "Please don't insult my toughness like that. I'm only out of breath from you pressing close to me and me wanting to kiss you even longer than I did downstairs."

Her mouth dropped open. "Are you serious?"

"Very." He lifted her off the ground and pressed her against the wall so their faces were close. His strong body and hands pinned her in place. "Kylee, can I kiss you longer than I did downstairs?"

Kylee could hardly believe this incredible man was so taken with her. He easily held her as if she weighed nothing. She'd seen the scale three mornings ago, before her life imploded. One-five-two. At five feet, that was considered overweight and very close to obese. Yes, she had generous curves and carried most of that weight in her chest and rear. Her waistline and even her legs were close to a normal-sized person, but how could Chandler be so attracted to her, hold her as if she weighed nothing? It blew her mind, and she loved him even more for it.

"You are some kind of superstar," she murmured against his mouth.

He grinned. "Please say that translates to, 'kiss me longer than you did downstairs.'"

Kylee laughed. She couldn't help it. She was caught up in the fairytale of her and Chandler Delta. She thought she loved him.

She listened, but no snarky voice came.

Chandler really was like a knight in shining armor. He'd killed the evil witch in her head.

"Yes," she said happily. "Please kiss me longer than you did downstairs, *el campeón*."

He chuckled. Then he kissed her, and she forgot to care about any insecurities. She even pushed aside the worries of confronting Mimi and King Frederick and possibly being killed in less than forty-eight hours. Chandler was all she could see, taste, smell, and feel. Chandler was all that mattered.

Chapter Twelve

Chandler was flying high the next morning from his kisses with Kylee. He'd finally let her get some rest, but she'd seemed as reluctant to pull away as he had. Did she care for him as deeply as he did for her? The only thing he would change about last night was he wished she'd responded to him when he'd bared his soul and been vulnerable, told her he was scared to get hurt again and told her she was the only woman for him. He knew she struggled with confidence and accepting compliments. Could he build her up and somehow show her all that he saw in her? She wasn't just gorgeous physically—her insides were beautiful too. She was pure, kind, and somehow unspoiled despite how awful her grandmother was.

The day went far too fast, and they were surrounded by people all the time. They had a big breakfast, then Papa wanted Colton and Bailey to help Chandler as he worked with Kylee on self-defense. That was a hit to his pride, which was silly. Colton was a successful doctor, but until he met Bailey last spring, he'd only focused on medicine and training to protect the secret. Chandler had shifted his focus to lacrosse at ten years old and though he'd tried to keep up with Delta protection, it hadn't been his top priority.

They actually had fun working with and teasing with Colton and Bailey. Papa had told them the tailor would sew in pockets to the dress that would be hidden at Kylee's hips as the dress would have more padding in the hips and chest to accentuate her small waist.

Kylee had muttered something about her huge chest and hips, but nobody but Chandler and Bailey, who were closest to her, had heard. Papa had continued speaking about the secret pocket underneath the actual pockets that would have a knife in it. So they'd worked on training with knives as well.

Before he knew it, lunchtime had come and a lot of the family were around to talk and tease with. He couldn't get Kylee alone to tell her that her hips were perfect. He didn't dare say anything about her perfect chest. He knew the thin shape was in right now, but for him Kylee's generous curves were so appealing he had trouble thinking straight if he let himself focus on her shape too much.

After lunch, the tailor arrived and his mom and Kylee went into a bedroom with the guy from Denver. Papa trusted him not to ask questions. Chandler needed a little time to think and knew she'd be at least an hour, so he told Thor he was going on a quick trail run.

"Trying to clear your head?" Thor asked knowingly.

"Sadly yes. Kylee's got me all stirred up."

"Good woman." Thor slapped him on the back. "Don't worry, bro. She's into you. She's had a pretty rough time with her grandmother. It'll take time to build up her confidence, but a stud like you can do it."

Chandler thanked his brother and took off running into the mountains. How did Thor see the situation so clearly? Was it possible that Kylee's reluctance with him had nothing to do with her thinking he was a womanizer and everything to do with her grandmother belittling her when she was a teenager and had just lost her parents? That would be rough to heal from.

He lost track of time as he stewed about his and Kylee's relationship and how tomorrow night would go. He was terrified to think of Kylee getting hurt. Thankfully, Papa was going to allow him to be staged outside the party and move in if things went awry. He knew that was generous of Papa, as most of the other family members were better qualified. Even though his brothers teased him, all his family treated him like an equal and he knew better than to let his own confidence take a hit comparing himself to others.

He slowed his steps in the trees as he approached the end of the trail that would take him to the lake and the grass and Papa's backyard.

Walking and pulling in slower breaths, he made it to Papa's backyard. It was quiet at the moment. Everyone must've gone to their own homes for a bit. He heard voices around front and slowly walked that way. He recognized Kylee's voice instantly. She was talking to a man. He stopped and listened for a second.

"Did you *know* my best guy was the leading scorer in the NCAA as a freshman?" The man's voice was slightly off.

Chandler leaned closer. That voice was familiar, but not a family member. Who would know his stats that well?

"And he broke the record for most points in a season as a rookie in the PLL," Kylee came back with.

"So good! You know how fast his shot is?"

Chandler recognized that voice. It was Bentley Jardine, his friend from high school who was a bit slow mentally. Bentley was the greatest guy and had the biggest heart in the world. Greer had told Chandler that Bentley came over to watch his lacrosse games all the time and he was his biggest fan. It was fun to hear him and Kylee talking.

"Clocked at one-nineteen-point-four," Kylee said, obvious pride and excitement in her voice. "So close to Patrick Luehrsen's record."

"So close." Bentley sighed. "He beat it next time."

"I hope so. I've never missed watching a game," she said. "I love seeing him play."

"Me too," Bentley agreed.

Chandler was stunned by this conversation. Not by Bentley's words, but by Kylee's. She'd teased him about being a lacrosse superstar and alluded to seeing him play, but to know his stats and to have never missed a game? That was superfan status for sure. He was so happy right now.

He barely caught Bentley's next words as he hurried around the house, "My Chandler is such a stud. He gets *all* the pretty women." Bentley saw him and his face lit up. "Chandler! My man!"

Bentley rushed to him, clasped his hand, and then hugged him. Chandler returned the hug, pulling back first. He wanted to talk to Kylee so badly. She was turned slightly away from him, and he couldn't read her expression.

"I came to visit Greer and he say you were here!" Bentley crowed.

"Excuse me," Kylee said. "So nice to meet you, Bentley."

"You too, Kylee." Bentley waved happily.

"Wait," Chandler begged. She couldn't walk away right now.

"I need to use the bathroom," she said quickly.

"Oh." He had nothing to say to that.

She rushed away, and he watched her go.

"She's pretty," Bentley said, pumping his eyebrows.

Chandler laughed and slung his arm around Bentley's shoulder. "She's more than pretty, my friend."

"Uh-huh," Bentley agreed.

They got into a discussion on lacrosse and before Chandler knew it, he needed to go shower for dinner. Dinner was a noisy and fun affair, with Papa grilling steak and chicken kabobs and everyone talking and enjoying each other. He sat by Kylee, but she was definitely not herself. Bailey was on her other side and Chandler heard her ask quietly if she was nervous about tomorrow. Kylee admitted she was, and Chandler relaxed a bit. Whatever was going on wasn't her pulling away from him after their incredible re-connection and kisses last night. That was a relief.

The evening was fun, but then grew serious as Papa took those flying with them tomorrow to the conference room and went over everything from how they would incapacitate, without hurting, three of the servers closest to Klein, Reed, and Bailey's sizes, to the floor plan of the Seamons' home, with Kylee giving input whenever she was asked, to the fact that they still had no confirmation of help from the military or government. That was surprising with Papa's status and influence with the military, but everyone seemed terrified of Frederick's cache of nuclear weapons and was hesitant to rock the boat.

At this point, the vile dictator could probably stroll into the White House and the President would smile and shake his hand. It was sickening, and they had to somehow keep America safe with no backup. Nuclear winter was a terrifying prospect, so Chandler couldn't blame the politicians and military leaders for treading carefully. He had no idea of a solution to the issue. Frederick ruled with threats, intimidation, murder, and loads of financial backing. He kept hiring more and more mercenaries, offering money no military personnel had ever seen. There was some theorizing that China was funding him, and Chandler sure hoped that wasn't true. Frederick's troops were now fighting against Poland and Germany and nobody was making a move to help, bound by the fear of him launching his nukes.

As they finally finished and the group dispersed, Papa asked them all to get some rest as they'd leave for the airport in Denver at eight a.m. the next morning.

Chandler and Kylee said goodnight to their family members and headed upstairs. He stopped by her bedroom door, hoping he could at least hold her and reassure her everything would be okay. But he was nervous. Frederick seemed untouchable. She only had to get the hair. He and Colton wondered if it had something to do with DNA and the weapon, but who knew?

"You all right?" he asked softly.

Her dark eyes flashed at him. "I'm fine, thank you. Goodnight."

Goodnight? What was going on?

Chandler placed his hands on either side of her shoulders, pinning her to the wall and preventing her from escaping. The warning in her eyes should've made him back up. "Kylee? What's going on?"

"Nothing. Just nervous about tomorrow."

He studied her. "Why are you pushing me away?"

"I'm pushing you away?" she asked. She pushed out a huffy breath. "After you overheard me reciting stats with Bentley, I thought your head would be so big you wouldn't believe the obsessed fan girl could ever push you away."

He shook his head. "I thought it was incredible that you knew my stats and have watched all my games."

"It's humiliating that you know that." She wouldn't meet his gaze.

"No, it's not," he insisted. "It's adorable. I love that you're an 'obsessed fan girl.'"

"Well, I don't," she shot back at him. "And it just means that I know Bentley is right and 'the stud' gets every woman he ever looks twice at. I've seen *all* the social media posts, Chandler."

"Ah, that's what's going on." He stared at her, bugged that she still thought he was some player. "Kylee. I've dated a lot of women." He wouldn't lie to her; dating wasn't a crime. "But no woman has ever compared to what I felt for you as an inexperienced sixteen-year-old."

"Don't try that with me."

"Excuse me?"

"I know you're a womanizer. Don't claim I'm special to you."

"Kylee." He shook his head in frustration. Why wouldn't

she believe him? "I am not some womanizer. I don't take advantage of women and then dump them. I treat women with respect. And you are special. You've always been the only one for me."

Her dark eyes seemed to soften.

He bent closer. "You're the most incredible and beautiful woman I've ever known."

Her jaw tightened. "And there you go with the empty compliments."

"Excuse me?" He straightened. "Empty compliments? I've meant every compliment I've ever given you."

Her jaw worked and her eyes brightened.

"When are you going to believe that I'm sincere about how taken with and invested in you I am? There is no one else for me, Kylee. No one."

She studied him, but then she gave an oddly nonchalant shrug.

Chandler's frustration grew. He understood she struggled with self-confidence because of her grandmother, but how could he convince her he was genuine? How could he get her to trust him?

He wasn't close to ready to give up. She was the one for him. "Kylee, please believe that I will not give up on us."

"Excuse me?" Fire flashed in her eyes. "You gave up on us before."

"What are you talking about?"

"You're just going to go back to your celebrity lifestyle after this is over."

"No, I won't." He threw his hands in the air and straightened.

"When will you finally believe that you're the one I want? You and only you."

"How about if you actually text me? One single time. Give me some piece of evidence that I really am special to you. Not just another girl to flirt with, kiss, then break my heart when you ghost me."

"What are you talking about?"

Her jaw hardened, and she glared at him. "I fell head over heels for you that summer visit. I know it was dumb and my parents and grandparents said I was too young to know I was in love, but I was. On the car ride to the Denver airport, I idealistically told them all that I loved you and was going to marry you someday."

He couldn't hide his smile. "You did? I love that." He gently touched her shoulder.

She flinched away from him, and he startled. "

You love that you broke my heart?" she demanded, folding her arms across her chest.

"I broke your heart?" He was completely confused. She was the one who'd written him off.

"You ghosted me. Never had the courtesy to even text me like you promised."

"What?" He was stunned and confused and angry. He was trying to forgive and forget the heartbreak of that summer and now she was claiming he was the one who ghosted her?

"I was heartbroken, Chandler. Completely heartbroken. Then my parents died, and I spent the next two years of high school living with Mimi and Grandpa and listening to Mimi belittle me nonstop." She looked up at him and a tear trickled from the corner of her eye and ran down her face. "I know I was just a fling for you back then and I'm terrified that's all I am now."

"Kylee." He tried to gather her close, but she leaned away from him. He tamped down the frustration. When he admitted that he'd never stopped loving her last night, she hadn't responded and now she was claiming it was he that had never texted? "I don't know what you're talking about. I never ghosted you. You were never a fling for me. I thought you were the one back then, and I feel it even more deeply now." He gazed down at her. "Do you believe me?"

She pulled away and wiped off the tear. "I don't know what to believe. How do I know you won't just ghost me again?"

His jaw hardened and he pushed a hand at his hair. "Kylee, I didn't ghost you. I texted you and you were the one that called it a 'fling' and then told me you had a boyfriend and to not text you again."

"Excuse me?" Her eyes flashed at him. "Now you're lying to me about it?"

He blinked down at her. "Lying? One of us definitely remembers this wrong."

"Do you have the text?" she challenged him.

He shook his head. "I was so mad and hurt that I deleted it and deleted your contact."

"Hmm. Convenient."

His jaw dropped. "You really think I'm lying to you?"

"*Sei un bugiardo,*" she hurled at him.

Chandler loved when she spoke in foreign tongues, but right now it frustrated him. "What does that mean?"

"You're a liar."

His eyebrows rose and his neck tightened. He didn't know that anyone had ever called him a liar.

"I've never had a boyfriend, *ever*, and I wouldn't have sent that text. I was head over heels for you." Her face reddened. She ducked under his arm and into her doorway. "This is all awkward and embarrassing. It's too much with what has to happen tomorrow. Please, just ... let me get through tomorrow."

She slammed the door in his face. Chandler was stunned and ... heartbroken. She'd called him a liar. How could she claim she hadn't sent that text?

He stood in the hallway for a while, trying to muddle it out in his mind and wanting to pound on her door and demand they talk it out. He was a hundred percent certain about what that text had said. It was imprinted on his mind. How could she possibly call him the liar?

Pacing the hallway, he didn't even know what to think. She claimed she hadn't sent that text and she thought he'd ghosted her. He blew out a heavy breath. How could he clear this up with no proof?

His head pounded as he paced and came up with no solution to their impasse. Could she have forgotten? There was no way he was remembering it wrong.

The only thing she was right about was that they needed to get through tomorrow night. Maybe then could figure out what had happened, but it hurt that he'd told her time and again how deeply he cared and she didn't seem to believe the truth about that any more than she did about the text.

Chapter Thirteen

Kylee had a hard time sleeping Thursday night as she stewed about Chandler. She'd been humiliated that he'd caught her spewing stats to his friend Bentley and then when Bentley had said his "buddy Chandler gets all the women," it had been a stark reminder to her of Chandler's famous player status. She'd let herself get so caught up in his delicious kisses and proclamations that she was the one for him she'd forgotten he was a flirt and a ditcher.

Then to have him lie and make up some story about her sending a text that she had a boyfriend and Chandler was just a fling. That made her furious.

In the middle of the night, it hit her. It was probably one of his other girlfriends that summer who had sent him that text and he had somehow associated it with Kylee. That made more sense.

She wished he would own up to ghosting her and beg her forgiveness. She was upset, confused, and filled with self-doubt.

How in the world was she going to stride into Mimi's party with her head held high when she felt so low from Chandler taking her so high with his kisses and sweet words and then lying to her? She had no idea.

The only good news was Mimi's snarky voice hadn't returned to her head. On some subconscious level, did she believe Chandler's sweet words? Had she been transformed by his all-encompassing kisses? It was a lot to think about, and if they couldn't trust each about texts or the lack thereof that happened ten years ago, she didn't know that they could have a future.

She finally fell asleep, and the next morning went by in a blur as they ate a quick breakfast, drove to Denver, and then loaded onto a chartered airplane. Chandler stayed close to her side, but neither of them said much. The pained and almost vulnerable look on his face made her want to believe him and apologize for calling him a liar. But she would definitely remember sending a text like that. She would remember if he'd made any contact with her at all. It all made no sense.

She dozed on the flight and before she knew it, they were in Chicago and driving to a rental home near Mimi's. It was a gorgeous house in the exclusive Winnetka, north of Chicago. It wasn't as big as Mimi's, but still a fancy and sprawling tan-brick mansion.

Her nerves ramped up. The party was less than four hours away. Bailey and Chandler both tried to get her to eat, but she was tied in knots. She tried to listen to all the instructions from Papa. She knew exactly how to pull the hair capturer from her pocket or purse and get Frederick's hair. Her small purse would have the backup hair capturer and a knife hidden, along with perfume, lip gloss, and all kinds of makeup and feminine products to dissuade any guard who might search her.

It all seemed surreal. Like she was in a Mission Impossible movie. Sadly, she felt like she was the weak link and would make this mission impossible. The only happy news was that Mimi's voice didn't make a snarky comment about that. It was wonderful to have her head clear of the bitter thoughts. If she and Chandler didn't have a future, at least he'd given her the gift of killing the evil witch in her head.

She went to get ready while most of the crew went with Papa to intercept the servers and get Bailey, Klein, and Reed into place. It helped strengthen her knowing those three would be in the house with her. If only it could be Chandler, but Mimi would instantly recognize any Delta and that would compromise the mission before it began. The Delta family could only come in if everything imploded and hiding their identity didn't matter any longer.

Bailey carefully applied all the makeup Myrna had provided her with, then slipped into the beautiful dress. Her hair was in long curls down her back and the pale blue, skin-tight gown with extra padding on the bustline, hips, and rear took her normally huge curves to gargantuan. Why anyone thought that was attractive, she'd never know, but everyone else believed it was, and believed it would get Frederick's attention. Luckily, the bodice was tight but didn't reveal too much skin or cleavage.

A rap came at the door. She looked at herself one more time in the mirror. She was ready.

No, she wasn't.

"Just a moment," she called.

"Okay," Chandler's voice called back.

Her heart sang just hearing his voice. She tried to tamp the feeling down. They both thought the other was a liar. He hadn't called her that, but she could see in his blue eyes that he thought it.

She'd thought they had issues they couldn't overcome with him being a player and her struggling to feel confident and the abrupt ending to their relationship as teenagers. The lying and misunderstandings just made it worse.

Carefully kneeling in the tight dress, she closed her eyes, bowed her head, clasped her hands and begged her father above, and her parents if they were listening, "Please protect all of us tonight. Please bless we can get the hairs from Frederick and that no one will be killed. Please bless I can hold my head high and be confident. Please bless I can forgive Chandler and know what to do about him. I know it's silly, but please bless me to feel attractive." She paused. It was silly. It shouldn't matter. But after believing Mimi's belittling words for years and then all the Deltas contradicting those words so strongly, especially Chandler, she really did feel pretty. If only Chandler wasn't also lying to her about their past.

She shook her head and focused. "Thank you that Mimi's voice isn't in my head anymore. Thank you for the Delta family, their training, their expertise, their kindness, and their willingness to protect me and the entire world. Thank you for Chandler. In the name of our Savior, amen."

She stayed on her knees, even though the tile wasn't comfortable. Peace washed over her and for just this moment, she thought it would all work out.

Forcing herself to stand, she grabbed the little purse and

strapped it over her shoulder, patted the pocket where the knife and small vial were, and walked to the door. Her heels were four inches. She was good at walking in heels—even her tennis shoes had heels—so it should be no big deal, but she was teetering. No matter the peace she'd felt, no matter that Chandler and his family had given her confidence that she thought she'd never had. She was still terrified. Terrified of facing Mimi and Frederick. Even more terrified of losing Chandler.

She grabbed the door handle, threw back her shoulders, pasted on a brilliant smile, and opened the door.

Chandler was standing there. He looked incredible in a fitted black T-shirt and black pants, his arm muscles pronounced and his blue eyes piercing. He'd be part of the special ops crew with his brothers Aiden, Thor, and Greer and his cousin Colton. With men like this around, how dare she be afraid?

His mouth fell open and his blue eyes filled with appreciation and warmth. "Kylee ..." His voice was almost worshipful as he slowly looked her over. "You are so exquisitely beautiful."

Her brilliant smile faded to a shy one. He seemed so sincere. How could she doubt him? How could she not just pull him in and kiss him until he knew he was far more beautiful than anyone to her?

"Thank you," she managed. "Is it time?"

He shook his head and took a step closer. "Papa and the rest of the guys aren't back yet. They'll be here soon and fit you with the earpiece, camera, and mic."

"Okay." She drew in a breath and put her free hand to her stomach. "It all feels so surreal."

"I bet. Are you feeling all right? I hate to have you be the one going in there."

She put her hand on his arm and savored the feel of his firm flesh. He looked at her hand, then back at her.

"I'm okay, Chandler. I just prayed and I ... I feel like it's going to work out. Somehow."

"I've been praying too," he admitted. He eased in closer yet again and she could've backed farther into the room, but she stood her ground and looked up at his clear blue eyes. With her heels on, she was a bit closer to his handsome face.

He gently cupped her cheek and said in a gravelly voice, "I've been praying you'll all be safe."

"Thank you."

"And I've been praying that you will know without any shadow of doubt how beautiful, incredible, and impressive you are to me."

Her eyes widened at that. She should move away, but his gaze and hand captivated her.

"And I've been praying that you will believe I'm telling you the truth that I sent a text all those years ago."

He didn't say more about her return text, but she couldn't help but ask, "Could one of your other girlfriends have sent that text and you confused us?"

His blue eyes widened in disbelief. "Kylee, I wasn't dating anyone else that summer. It was you. It's always been you for me."

She stared at him, and she believed him. At least that she was the only one he'd been dating that summer. Biting her lip, she said, "I want to believe you about not ghosting me, but trust me, I would remember. You were my every hope and dream. So much in my life would have been different if ....”

His gaze got intense, and he said, “Kylee, could someone else have taken your phone, sent that text, and then deleted the text stream and blocked my number?”

She stared at him. “Why would someone ...” Her own eyes widened as the truth hit her like a punch in the gut. It was instantly clear, and she couldn’t believe she hadn’t seen it before.

“Mimi,” she muttered darkly, upset at herself for not thinking of that possibility sooner. Of course. Mimi would do anything to hurt Kylee.

“It’s the only explanation I can come up with,” he said. “Because I remember clearly the moment I texted you. I went to that spot we found along the creek, where the water sounded like music over the stones. It took me way too long to compose the perfect text. And even though I got a text back that hurt worse than a lacrosse ball to the face, I believe you when you say that you never saw it and that you didn’t send the breakup text.”

“Wow. I can’t believe she would ... yet I can.”

She tried to think it through. In the Denver airport, she remembered running to get some food for the flight with her parents while Mimi and Grandpa stayed with the luggage. Kylee’s phone had been sitting in her backpack. Mimi had been complaining that they couldn’t get a chartered flight and how she hated being around all these ... lower-class citizens. It had ticked her dad off, so her mom had suggested the three of them go get food. Mimi must have heard a text alert and pulled the phone out. She’d used her dad’s birth year for every four-digit code and Mimi had known that.

After her parents' deaths, Mimi and Grandpa's financial situation had completely changed. She'd always assumed Mimi had taken all the life insurance money to support her affluent lifestyle, but even that wouldn't have been enough. She believed now that Mimi had sold her soul for wealth and influence.

"I'm sorry I called you a liar," she said quietly.

Doors opened and closed downstairs and footsteps and voices floated up.

"Thank you." Chandler leaned in and wrapped his free arm around her waist. "I pray you can believe that I would never ghost the most important woman in the world to me, but more importantly, I pray you can know how perfect you are. You're more than enough, Kylee. Please don't believe anything your grandmother tried to feed you. Please believe that in my eyes you're the most incredible woman ever created, and I want you to be by my side always. I want you to be my everything. And I pray I can be there to protect, love, and cherish you."

The words were so beautiful, but also so big. She'd fallen in love with Chandler at sixteen, but she had always tried to convince herself it was just a shallow teenage relationship. It had been the only way for her to reconcile it in her mind when she thought he'd dumped her.

She wanted to tell him she loved him, but she was overwhelmed. She was still trying to process that he hadn't ghosted her, that Mimi had done another evil deed that had adversely affected her life, and that Chandler cared for her every bit as much as she cared for him.

Chandler looked her over and murmured softly, *"Belle, hermosa, bellissima, linda."*

"Oh, Chandler." Her breath caught in her throat and her heart raced. She loved, loved that he'd learned beautiful in French, Spanish, Italian, and Portuguese.

He smiled, but then his blue eyes grew serious. "And just to show you there's no doubt that I'm sincere ..." He bowed his head and captured her lips with his own. The kiss was intense and robbed her of all coherent thought and oxygen. She leaned into him and he deepened the kiss.

"Kylee, Chandler ... oh." Aiden's voice was far too close for comfort.

Chandler released her from the kiss, but cuddled her tight to his perfect chest. She looked over and Aiden was at the top of the stairs.

"Sorry to interrupt, but it's time." His voice held a teasing note.

"We're coming," Chandler told him, not taking his eyes off of Kylee.

Kylee was grateful that the Deltas all seemed so confident about tonight. She eased back and blew out a breath. "Here we go."

He nodded.

Her mind was full of so many things. She loved Chandler but didn't know if she was ready to tell him that. She had to fully process that Mimi had broken them up at sixteen and then programmed Kylee's mind to believe she was unattractive and unwanted. It had sadly worked. So many years she'd let Mimi control her, even though she'd moved out at eighteen and claimed Mimi had no control over her. It frustrated her that though she'd thought she was strong and independent, she'd never let go of that nagging Mimi voice and influence. Not until last night when Chandler had interrupted the voice, telling her how beautiful she was inside and out and kissing her so thoroughly.

He was incredible.

Chandler took her hand and walked her to the stairs, following Aiden down. She wished she could gush about how she felt about him and plan a future together, but this wasn't that moment. The world's safety was riding on her getting some hairs. It was insane. Somehow she had to get through this op, and in the process she had to prove to herself she could stand up to Mimi, and they all had to survive.

The next hour was a whirlwind of being fitted with the mic and camera on the jewels of her bodice and the earpiece that she'd learned how to quietly listen and speak into without touching it.

They made it to Mimi's house and her nerves ramped up again as Chandler drove her up to the front door in an older Lexus with an Uber sticker in the window. High end cars were parked in the huge circle drive, most of them with drivers waiting for their important guests.

As they stopped, Chandler glanced into the rearview. "You've got this, Kylee. You're strong, brave, beautiful, and my entire family is praying nonstop for you, most of all me."

She smiled back at him, but the doorman was opening her door. "Thanks," was all she managed to get out to Chandler.

He inclined his chin to her, and his blue eyes filled with a fierce protectiveness. She pitied the person who tried to hurt her if Chandler was anywhere close by. She'd never felt so safe and protected, and she was walking into the lioness's den. It made no sense.

She took the doorman's hand and stepped out, relieved to see it was Jason, an older gentleman who had served Mimi at parties where she wanted to look uppity for years.

"Jason," she said, genuine delight in her voice.

"Miss Seamons." Jason blinked down at her. "You are an absolute vision."

"Thank you."

He closed the door and escorted her up the long, flower-lined walk. She barely resisted looking back at Chandler.

It was a mild night in Chicago for early September, so she wasn't cold in her sleeveless dress. Despite the balmy weather, Mimi would make the gardener cover the flowers each night to keep them alive as long as possible.

She heard Chandler drive off and felt bereft for a second.

"You've got this, beautiful," Chandler's voice said in her earpiece.

Kylee smiled and kept her shoulders straight. She did have this. She said another prayer for help and let Jason lead her up the walk.

"Forgive me, sweet girl, but Mrs. Seamons did not inform me you were expected tonight," Jason said. She knew he would have a guest list and if there was any deviation, security would be on that person in an instant.

She glanced to the side and saw men in suits stationed in the shadows of the gabled porch. They'd have weapons, and they wouldn't be afraid to bodily escort anybody far from the premises. Especially with King Frederick here tonight.

She thought of Chandler holding her close, telling her she was incredible.

She could do this.

"I've been out of town and didn't tell them I was coming back. I wanted to surprise them." She squeezed Jason's arm. "Grandpa will be thrilled, don't you think?"

If only that was still true.

Jason nodded. His eyes looked leery and her chest squeezed. He was going to keep her out. "Will Mrs. Seamons ...?"

"She'll like the surprise," Kylee reassured. "She had someone she wanted me to meet tonight and was royally ticked off when I told her I couldn't come."

"Ah." Jason understood what that meant. "She's decided to pair you off." He smiled like a loving grandfather. If only her own grandfather loved her. "Well, whoever it is will be instantly smitten with you in this dress."

"I hope so." Kylee forced a laugh. Mimi had never tried to set her up, always telling her she wasn't attractive enough for a man to notice her. Now Kylee knew she was wrong. Chandler was the most attractive man on the planet, and he wanted her and only her. It was easy to put a radiant smile on her face with a devoted love like Chandler's backing her up.

Jason opened the door and informed his younger counterpart, a smiling young man named Miles. "Please see Miss Seamons into the gathering area while I greet any other latecomers."

Kylee breathed easier even as Miles looked her over like a wolf.

"Of course," he said. He took her arm and Jason shut the door behind them. "Wow, Kylee. You look incredible."

"Thank you." She placed her hand on his arm and let him escort her through the huge foyer to the even more massive gathering area on the right.

The crowd was large, which was good. It was large enough she could blend in, get what she needed, then get out. But not large enough that she couldn't find her target.

She lifted her hand from Miles' arm and thanked him, then started working her way through the crowd, saying hello to her grandparents' friends and some military people she'd known her entire life. Everyone was happy to see her and very complimentary. She had a confidence that felt like it was coming from heaven and from Chandler.

There were other people she didn't know personally, but some she recognized, senators and judges who should not be mingling with the likes of King Frederick. But there you were ...

She saw her grandmother, grandfather, and the self-proclaimed King close to the rear wall in a greeting line of sorts. "I see the target," she said quietly.

"I'm going to serve him a drink in just a moment," Bailey said. "Do you want to wait and see if I can manage it then?"

"No. I've got this." Kylee put all the confidence that her prayer, Chandler's words, and Chandler's kisses had given her into her voice. Then she stepped into the line of people waiting to talk to her grandparents and the king. Her heart picked up a beat and she second-guessed her brave words. Did she have this? Or would Mimi best her, tear her to the ground, and belittle her into submission just as she had since Kylee was sixteen and her parents died?

The line moved forward. Kylee felt the self-doubt creep back in. Her palms grew clammy and her feet felt like lead blocks. She looked down at her voluptuous body spilled into this tight dress and could already imagine the cutting comments her grandmother would make for all to hear. Could she really do this? She looked back at the arched entry, tempted to run as fast as she could in these spike heels and too-tight dress.

If she did, maybe she'd be a distraction and Bailey could finish the job. But would she ever forgive herself for wimping out? Would she ever be enough for Chandler if she couldn't stand up to her grandmother once and for all and prove that she was confident, brave, smart, and beautiful? At least she was to the one man who mattered most to her.

Chandler.

She put a hand to her racing heart and said another desperate prayer for help.

Chapter Fourteen

Praying nonstop for strength, Kylee opened her eyes to see Bailey not too far away. Her beautiful friend was wearing a simple white blouse and a black skirt with her hair in a bun. She was still beautiful, but King Frederick wouldn't spare her a second glance as a server. Kylee looked down at her shiny dress and she suddenly had the strangest vision. It was as if she were seeing herself from the outside. Her shape was just as rounded and crazy out of proportion as it had always been—actually more so with the extra padding on her bustline and hips to hide the mic, camera, knife, and extra hair-gatherer. The thing was, she could see that her curves were smooth and eye-catching, and her face and hair looked gorgeous, especially her dark eyes that seemed to sparkle.

She knew exactly why they were sparkling. She was a woman in love, and her man more than returned that love. He would do anything to protect her and help her see how she appeared to him. He loved her from the inside out.

"You've got this, *bellissima*," Chandler said in her earpiece.

She wanted to scream that she loved him and tell him thank you a million times for helping to infuse her with the confidence she felt right now. A confidence that wouldn't dim because she finally believed every incredible word he'd said to her. He was her everything, and if she lived through tonight, she was going to tell him that and kiss him for a very, very long time.

She gave generous, fake smiles to the men who ogled her and noticed Klein and Reed moving through the party, getting their share of feminine wanton glances as they served appetizers. She was so glad they were inside the house with her.

The line moved slowly forward and her nerves grew, but her confidence didn't wane like it normally would knowing she'd face her grandmother soon. Interesting that she wasn't afraid of the murderous, conniving dictator. She was pretty certain the man had nothing on her grandmother. She opened her purse and reapplied her lip gloss, then as she put it away, she stealthily pulled out the little hair-gathering contraption and slid out the end that would rip out Frederick's hair, putting the container back in her purse. Her hands didn't even shake. She thanked heaven above.

"Kylee's moving in," she heard Reed say in the earpiece. She was glad there wasn't constant chatter in her ear. That would've made it hard to concentrate.

"We're right here for you," Papa said.

"You've got this, Kylee." Chandler's voice.

"I do," she whispered back.

One more person in front of her, but her grandmother was the first one she would reach, and she suddenly glanced her way. "Kylee," she muttered, her voice more snarky and mean than ever.

Kylee put on her most radiant smile. "Hello, Grandmother," she drawled out.

"It's *Mimi*," her grandmother all but shrieked.

People looked their way.

Mimi put on a fake smile and stepped around the person in front of Kylee, grabbing her arm. "What are you doing here, you ungrateful brat?" Before Kylee could answer, she looked her over. "All squeezed into that dress, aren't you? Good heavens, darlin', try out a salad and the treadmill for once in your lazy life."

Kylee heard a growl in her earpiece, then a warning of, "Chandler."

She smiled to herself. He would stand up for her, but it was time to stand up for herself. "Ah, *Grandmother*." She looked her up and down as outrage filled Mimi's dark gaze. "I know how jealous you are of my beauty and my shape." As she said the words and looked into her grandmother's hate-filled gaze, she realized it was true. Her grandmother was so stuck trying to be the most beautiful woman around that she couldn't even handle her own granddaughter being beautiful. Mimi's insane jealousy had fueled all the hateful and belittling words throughout the years.

"That's right, *belle*," Chandler said in her ear, giving her even more strength.

Mimi gasped, but Kylee wasn't done. They were gathering a crowd. She didn't care.

"I am finished with you trying to belittle me and finished with you sending your man to kill me. I am a beautiful and successful adult ... and I am through with you."

Mimi's eyes narrowed but Kylee pushed past her, easily

shoving her too-thin, plastic-face and silicone-parts grandmother out of the way.

"*Hallo, König Frederick.*" Kylee greeted him with a huge smile, as if he was the most important man in her world.

"*Schön,*" he drawled out *beautiful* in German. Frederick was a short but powerfully built man. He looked like a square tank. He had thick dark hair, piercing dark eyes, and a full beard. He appeared much taller on television.

She put out her right hand for him, catching a glimpse of her grandfather on the other side, begging her with his gaze to run. She could feel her grandmother fuming on her right. She smiled at her grandfather when she wanted to tell him off as well. He was too weak to waste her time on.

Frederick grasped her hand and brought it to his lips. His beard tickled her fingers, but not in a good way. Her stomach turned over as he kissed her hand, and then he trailed his tongue along her knuckles. Gross. It was all she could do to not pull her hand free and smack him.

He straightened, staring deeply at her as if he could possess her with his eyes. "I have bowed to your beauty," he said in heavily accented English. "I have not seen your equal in this country. Who are you, and how can I convince you to come home with me?"

Kylee heard a very loud growl in her ear and another reprimand of "Chandler." She teetered on her heels but focused on heavenly protection and all the Deltas being close at hand.

"I am Admiral and Olivet Seamons' only granddaughter, Kylee," she said, her head erect and her smile in place. She stepped in close, lifting her left hand as if to embrace him.

He tugged her closer with his right hand that still held hers.

She all but fell against his powerful body. With her heels on, she was only an inch shorter than him.

Resisting the urge to vomit, Kylee ran her fingertips through his hair and then leaned close to his ear, she blew air into his ear at the same time that she pushed the small contraption hidden in her left palm against the back of his head and then ripped it back.

He jerked in surprise at the tug to his hair, but she tried to keep his focus as she stayed close to him and whispered in his ear, "Come find me after you're done greeting people. We'll chat about what's in store for our future."

She eased back to see him beaming at her. Apparently her words and her closeness had kept him from thinking the tug to his hair was anything more than her playing with him. Her stomach was pitching so hard she had to swallow to keep the vomit down. She smoothly cupped her left hand around the hair.

"I will find you," he said. "That is a promise, *meine liebe.*"

Thankfully, he released her before she used her new self-defense moves to prove to him she would never be "his love."

She winked at Frederick and said, "*Bis gleich.*" *See you soon.* Not. Then she tilted her chin to her grandfather as if he were below her. "Grandfather."

Spinning on her heels, she strutted away from the three of them. She quickly slipped the hair catcher back into the attachment and into her purse, zipping it shut. The crowd parted for her to go.

"Get out of there," Papa instructed her in her ear. "Klein, Reed. Close in on Kylee's location."

She needed no prodding.

Suddenly, a scream went up. "She's got a gun!"

Kylee whirled to see Mimi pointing a gun at her, rage filling her features.

"I own you, and you'll never be more beautiful than me!" Mimi screamed.

"Olivet?" King Frederick questioned.

"No!" her grandfather yelled.

Mimi was completely focused on Kylee. The small handgun in her grip was aimed at Kylee's heart. People scrambled to get away from Kylee even as she heard many voices in her ear and saw Klein and Reed sprinting in her direction. Reed yanked a gun out of his suit pocket, but he couldn't stop Mimi.

A body flew into Kylee, knocking her to the ground as Mimi's gun discharged. A second gun went off and Kylee heard a shriek from her grandmother and a thud.

Warm liquid oozed onto her thigh where the slit had been pushed up. She looked at her rescuer. "Grandpa?"

He smiled wanly at her. His face was pale and blood oozed from his leg. "Lucky for us, she's a terrible shot," he said.

"Why would you save me?" she rushed out. "The jade necklace you gave me led the hitman straight to me."

"It was a tracking device?" Grandpa shook his head. "Oh, my girl, I didn't know that. Olivet must've had the jeweler add that."

Kylee had no clue if she could trust him, but he had saved her life.

Mimi was shrieking as Reed, Klein, and Bailey descended on her. "Don't touch me, you foul serving people," she hollered.

Reed stripped the gun from her trembling hand as Klein took the clean towel Bailey gave him, kneeled, and pressed it against the blood seeping from her right shoulder.

"We're trying to help you, you pompous witch," Bailey snapped.

"Help me! He shot me," she screamed, pointing at Reed. "Security!"

Other people were milling around, not seeming to know what to do, looking around for the security as well.

"You'll find your security has been detained." Reed gave her grandmother a smirky grin.

"What? How dare you!" Mimi screamed louder still.

Bailey came toward Kylee and her grandfather with another clean towel. Her grandpa rolled off her and onto the ground, lying on his back as Bailey put pressure on the wound and spoke into her mic. "We've got two wounded. Neither life threatening."

"Kylee!" The yell came from the entryway.

Kylee looked, and there he was. Chandler ran for her, and the crowd parted to let him through. She struggled to her knees—blast this tight dress.

Chandler reached her, his blue eyes full of concern and love for her. He easily lifted her off the ground and against his chest. She was safe and she was loved and she was more than enough. She knew all of that from the strength he infused into her.

"You're not hurt?" he asked urgently.

"No." She shook her head.

He bent and captured her mouth with his, kissing her deeply and thoroughly and leaving her no doubt that he was enraptured by her and that he loved her.

"No!" Mimi was screaming. "You can't have her! I forbid her to love a Delta!"

Chandler pulled back slightly and met Kylee's gaze. His blue eyes captivated her. "Do you?" he asked. His voice got lower and there was a vulnerability in his gaze that made her love him even more. He loved her, and he understood her self-doubts, and he would build her up and strengthen her any time she needed it. "Love a Delta?"

"Oh, Chandler." She cupped his jaw with her free hand, her right still clutching the small purse that held the valuable hair. "I love you more than anyone in this entire world. I want you to be my world."

Chandler grinned and then he was kissing her again.

When they pulled apart, she finally noticed that police were filtering onto the scene, the guests were being herded into different rooms for questioning, and EMTs were working on both of her grandparents.

She took Chandler's hand, and he grinned at her. "Do you want to get out of here?" he asked.

"Yes, please. I never want to walk into this house again."

"We can easily make that happen."

The EMTs rolled her grandfather past before Kylee and Chandler could walk away.

"Please stop," he begged.

Kylee looked down at him. Her heart swelled with love for him, even though she wasn't certain if he'd betrayed her or not.

"Kylee. All these years, I stayed with her to protect you."

"Excuse me?" Kylee was stunned.

He nodded. "I did the best I could to keep you safe, but Olivet is ... the devil."

Kylee smiled at that. "We can agree on that for sure."

Chandler's hand wrapped around her waist. She smiled up at

him, then watched as they wheeled her grandfather away. She'd talk to him some more. After she had a little more time to figure out the truth.

She looked back to where the EMTs were loading Mimi onto a stretcher. She should've left it alone, but she marched over to her. "Did you send a text to Chandler from my phone at the Denver airport after we went to visit the Deltas when I was sixteen?"

Mimi's plastic face couldn't move, but her eyes spewed hatred. "Yes," she hissed. Then she groaned as the EMTs wrapped her shoulder. "I knew if you loved a Delta I wouldn't be able to control you."

"Your plan failed." She looked up at Chandler, who was fully focused on her. "I love Chandler Delta," she said loudly. She glanced back at her grandmother. "And you have no control over me in any way, shape, or form."

Turning, she walked away, cuddled into Chandler's side.

Papa was right there. "King Frederick disappeared in all the commotion," he told them grimly. "Some guests claim he slipped out a patio door when Olivet pulled the trigger."

"Figures," Chandler said. "What a coward."

"Did you get the hair?" Papa asked.

"Of course." Kylee gave him a confident grin and then pulled the little vial out of her purse and handed it over.

Papa took it and gave her a soft kiss on the forehead. "You're incredible, Kylee. I'm proud to know you'll be part of our family."

She flushed with warmth at that idea. "Slow down, Papa. This stud has to impress me first." She winked at Chandler.

Chandler grinned.

Papa laughed. "Well, this superstar grandson of mine will

sweep you off your feet. I'm sure of that." He looked them over. "You two are going to be a power couple. You'll change the world in positive and uplifting ways. I couldn't be prouder of both of you."

Kylee hugged him and then Chandler got a hug from his Papa.

Papa put the vial in his suit pocket and headed to talk to a man in a Naval uniform.

Chandler turned Kylee back into him. "I don't want to rush you … but I can't imagine a world without you by my side."

Kylee grinned. "Slow down, my superstar lacrosse player … I just admitted I've loved you for over ten years. This is nothing we can rush." She laughed, so happy right now.

Chandler chuckled, and then he kissed her. Wow, did he kiss her!

The world lit up. All that mattered was Chandler.

She'd never felt so cherished or so beautiful.

Chapter Fifteen

Kylee stood in the stands at Subaru Park in Philadelphia. It was the Premier Lacrosse League championship game. Boston was up fourteen to seven with seconds left in the fourth quarter, and her superhero was just showing off at this point. She stood in the front row, screaming along with Papa and all of Chandler's immediate family and in-laws or future in-laws. Everyone except Hudson.

Joseph and Holly's family had offered to stay home and take care of everything in the valley, but more importantly protect the secret. Esther's fiancé Reed, the sheriff, had also decided to stay back and have his department help him monitor and protect the secret as well. His men didn't know exactly what they were patrolling for, but they willingly did whatever Reed asked.

King Frederick had escaped the night of the fateful party and seemed focused on his wars with Poland and Germany, but they all knew the man had plans for world domination and it was spooky to think the only thing stopping him from launching nuclear bombs at America was the Delta secret weapon that he didn't want to destroy. So the Delta family was all on high alert and as soon as this game was over, she and Chandler would head for Colorado with the rest of the family.

Everyone who attended the party was under quiet investigation, but so far no leads had come from it.

Her grandmother was currently in prison awaiting trial for attempted murder. Her grandfather had never been prosecuted and was still claiming Olivet had orchestrated everything, their marriage had deteriorated, and he had no affiliation with her or any of her schemes. Their house had been repossessed by the government, and any accounts associated with Olivet had been seized.

They had discovered that Nelson Palmer, who had sent Emery's brother Travis, his own son, and another of Travis's friends after the secret had actually been Olivet's secret lover. So gross, but it made sense. She'd been paid millions of dollars by Frederick to get the secret and had done everything in her power to do so. In prison, she kept screaming about Davidson Delta hiding a weapon, but everyone admired Papa Delta and believed him when he said she was insane.

It was easy to believe Olivet Seamons was insane.

"Go Chan!" Esther screamed from next to Kylee as Chandler caught the ball, spun around one defender, then pushed his backside into another, shoving the man toward the goal as he progressed that direction.

The crowd started counting down. "10, 9, 8 ..."

Chandler twisted around his defender and drilled the ball into the bottom left corner of the net.

The crowd went insane as the buzzer sounded.

Kylee screamed herself hoarse and took turns hugging each of their family members. Chandler and his teammates gave the other team handshakes and hugs and then they took a turn around the stadium, slapping hands with fans.

All the family hung over the railing to slap their hands. Chandler approached and his family went nuts. Grinning, he slapped each of their hands until he got to Kylee.

She batted her eyelashes at him. "Can I have your jersey, number eighty-three?"

He laughed, whipped off his jersey, and handed it to her. Kylee started laughing too, pinching the sweaty thing between her fingertips. "I love you, but I'm not putting that on."

Everybody around them laughed as Kylee draped it over a stadium chair.

"Hey, bros," Chandler said to Aiden and Thor. "Do me a solid and lift my girl to me?"

"Of course," Thor said.

Before Kylee could do anything, she was swept off her feet and lifted over the barrier and into Chandler's arms. She wrapped her arms around his neck, and even though he was sweaty, she couldn't resist cuddling into him.

"*Belle, hermosa, bellissima, linda,*" he whispered for only her to hear. He kissed her softly and then asked, "When all this craziness with the secret settles, will you go to St. Lucia with me and elope?"

Her eyes widened. "How did you know I've always wanted to go to St. Lucia?"

St. Lucia and Chandler? *Yes please!*

"I'm just that good," he said, smiling to himself.

"You actually are," she admitted to him. "*Oui, s'il-vous-plait, bien entendu, snalla, natuurlijk, niinpa tietysti, tottakai—*"

Chandler laughed. "Please say all of those mean, 'yes, take me away and marry me, my handsome love.'"

She winked. "That is exactly what they mean."

"Perfect." His blue eyes captivated her, telling her she was the only woman in the world for him. Then he bowed his head, and he kissed her.

The world lit up. She couldn't get enough of him.

Chandler Delta, the man she'd loved since she was sixteen, had helped her change her opinion about herself. He had showed her what true love really meant. He was her *amor verdadero* and her *el campeón*. Her everything.

Excerpt - Accepted - Delta #8

Lieutenant Braden Moyle glanced over his shoulder for what felt like the twentieth time tonight. It was a mild seventy degrees on a mid-September evening in Chicago. He was walking to his home near the Great Lakes Naval Base after a nice date with an attorney he'd met a few weeks ago. Somebody had been trailing them all night, maybe that was why the dinner conversation and even axe-throwing after was lackluster. He'd been pretty distracted trying to figure out why he'd been seeing Delta-family blue eyes all night. He'd also gotten glimpses of long, blond hair, but he didn't have a complete picture or more than a feeling that he was being followed. Whoever it was, they were good at shadowing.

Since he'd made a fateful trip to Summit Valley Colorado with some buddies a few months ago his life had changed a bit. He'd received a couple promotions and was now Lieutenant. He'd been offered a much higher housing stipend and moved out of the barracks into his own little home in a nice neighborhood close to base, shopping, and restaurants. He wasn't complaining about the benefits and he knew he worked hard and had earned them. Still he couldn't help but wonder if retired Admiral Davidson Delta had anything to do with his career going so well, or if it was all Admiral Seamons, Braden's CO and a man he admired as much as his own dad and grandpa.

His mind was full of the Deltas tonight. He hadn't been able to get the former Admiral Delta's piercing blue eyes out of his mind nor rid himself of the eerie feeling that Braden wasn't done with the Delta family or the secret he'd stupidly tried to go after.

He'd steered clear of everything Delta after that trip to Colorado. He'd promised Admiral Delta that he would and Braden had been taught from birth on up by his incredible parents that honesty and integrity were of utmost importance.

And now somebody was trailing him. He worried it was about the Deltas because of the blue eyes. He was pretty certain it was a woman. He wanted to stop and confront whoever it was. He walked casually around to his back door, avoiding the front porch that was lit up from the street. The person was still out front so he unlocked the back door, loudly banged open the door, flipped on the laundry room light, walked in place, and then shut the door.

Sliding off the back porch stoop into the shadowy spot next to his door, he leaned against the wall and hoped they wouldn't glimpse his outline. He wished he'd carried a weapon on his date, but who would've thought an innocent dinner and axe-throwing with a woman who almost hit herself with the axe, would lead to him waiting to see if his shadow would break into his house.

Within seconds he was rewarded by an average-height, fit woman in dark clothing with a long, blond ponytail setting a duffel and a purse on the ground, and then stepping onto the back porch stoop. She pulled a couple slim tools from her pocket, he assumed to break into the house.

He almost grabbed her then, but wanted to see how far she'd go. She was familiar to him and a tingling sensation told him this was what he'd been waiting for the past four months. The Deltas had sent someone after him. Why? They didn't trust him?

After Admiral Seamons' wife had been arrested only a few days ago, he'd been uneasy and wondered if something more was coming. Especially with rumors surrounding the arrest of Olivet Seamons actually being in cahoots with King Frederick, the dictator who was trying to take over Europe. It was heavy and he worried for Admiral Seamons. He hadn't thought he should be worried for himself. What had changed the status quo with the Deltas and had the former-Admiral send somebody after him?

The blonde tried the door handle and it turned in her hand. "Trusting and hot," she muttered, "Wish I could keep this one."

Braden's eyebrows rose. Was she talking about him? Who was this woman?

Sliding her tools back into a small pouch at her waist, she revealed a 1911 pistol strapped next to the pouch and Braden's blood ran colder. Was she sent to kill him? He'd done nothing but work hard, keep his nose down, and be loyal to his country and the Navy since his one indiscretion of going after the Delta secret for a fun adventure. Why would they send someone now? Could this person work for King Frederick and have found his connection to the Deltas? He would've thought that was far-fetched but Frederick seemed to have far too many loyal lackeys and spies. Braden had even heard rumors that Admiral Seamons' wife was not the only one in cahoots with King Frederick. And he'd heard rumors that Frederick was after retired Admiral Davidson Delta. Though the people who'd philosophized about that didn't know why, Braden thought he might. What was the Deltas secret and how was it going to affect him?

All of a sudden the woman's body seemed to stiffen. He tried to take shallower breaths. Had she heard him? He wished he could get a glimpse of her face. Should he disable her now? Take her gun and find out why she was breaking into his house?

Before he could decide if he should make his move now, or after she'd gone into his house, she pivoted, and leapt at him.

He stumbled back in surprise. The woman plowed into him, knocking him flat on his back. The breath was knocked out of him. He'd been taught to respect and protect women, but he wasn't going to let her take him down, or possibly kill him that easily.

He did a reversal and flipped her onto her back, pinning her down with his much heavier body and trapping her hands above her head.

The light from the porch illuminated her face, and what a face it was. She was stunningly beautiful and she looked almost exactly like Jessica Delta, a sweet girl he'd met in Colorado that fateful weekend. Except this woman was blonde not brunette. She could've died her hair though. There was something different about this Delta woman's eyes as well. They were not as innocent as Jessica's. As if she'd seen much more of the world than she wanted to.

"Well hello handsome," the woman he had pinned down said

with a teasing smirk on her face. "That's one way to get my attention."

"Jessica? Or her sister?" he ventured, loosening his grip on her but not lifting his weight off of her.

She laughed, a deep, throaty chuckle that somehow made him feel all lit up inside, despite the crazy circumstance he found himself in. He was certain now it wasn't Jessica, but this was one of the Delta family for sure. He forced himself to ignore the incredible sensation of being so close to this beautiful and intriguing woman. His racing pulse and quickened breath might reveal how attracted he was to her. He was certain this astute woman noticed both.

"Good guess," he said. "Jessie is my baby sis, a straight-up angel, and way too nice to do this."

She ripped one of her hands free and slugged him hard in the side of the abdomen. Braden grunted in surprise.

She didn't give him enough reprieve to grab her hand, but hit him in the same spot again. The hit was so brutal he wondered if she'd broken a rib. How had she learned to hit like that? He didn't want to hit a woman so he scrambled for her hand, tugged it back above her head, and pinned her down completely again.

"Stop," he told her sternly. "And tell me what you're doing here."

She smiled at him, a smile so sweet and alluring he was momentarily stunned. "That was me being kind, sailor. If you don't want me to insult and ruin your manhood I suggest you roll off of me right now."

Braden's eyes widened as he realized she could've kneed him instead of punched him. He obeyed and rolled off of her, but as he did, he ripped the 1911 from her hip holster. He popped to his feet and pointed it at her.

"Stand up nice and easy," he told her.

"That was a great move. Well done." The praise felt completely sarcastic. He had to hide a smile. She'd hold her own with his platoon.

She stood slowly, as if giving him time to appreciate how good she looked, and remember what it had felt like to pin her down. His pulse didn't slow down but he held his hand steady pointing the gun at her and he tried to look unphased. She was obviously used to men admiring her beauty. He could be reading her wrong but she seemed well-versed in tricking and having the upper hand with men as well.

She didn't bother to hold up her hands or act like he had the advantage in any way. "I'm Madison Delta," she said, her blue eyes all lit up as if they were bantering flirtatiously. "You can call me Maddie. My future sister-in-law Bailey told me what a gentleman you were." She paused and he easily remembered the fun and beautiful Bailey who'd ended up being part of his adventure-gone-wrong in Colorado. When the Deltas had captured them Braden tried to protect her, but she had bravely stood her own and Colton Delta had fallen in love with her.

"Jessie thought you were the 'sweetest man she'd ever met'," Maddie said, she fluttered her eyelashes as if she were a simpering debutante. He had no idea what to make of her. He didn't think she was making fun of her sister as much as she was teasing him. "She begged for this job but Papa knew my unique skill set would be essential." She winked. "Now I believe it's time for the two of us to go inside and get to know each other better. That'll be loads of fun." Her blue eyes glinted mischievously at him, "But I really don't like you *thinking* you have the upper hand."

"Well I do," he said, and thank heavens he did. He wasn't sure if he should laugh at her sassy teasing in such an odd and serious situation or if he should pin her down again and see if it felt as amazing as it had moments ago. If he pinned her down he could force her to tell him why she'd come for him. He'd been instructed to stay away from the Delta family and their secret and he'd honored his end of the deal. What had changed on their end?

"I'll decide if we 'get to know each other better'," he said. It would be fun to spend more time with this intriguing woman. Unfortunately he was certain her intentions had nothing to do with flirting with him or getting to know him. "Or if I have you arrested for breaking and entering and assault. How did you know everywhere I'd be tonight?"

She chuckled. "Oh, Lieutenant Moyle. There's something you need to wrap your mind around right up front and keep in mind throughout our exciting time spent together. The Delta family has more knowledge and clearance than anyone in any branch of the military, or the government. We also have better training and skills."

Leaping into the air, she kicked his hand so hard he felt like she broke a bone. The gun went flying into the grass. They both dove for it. Braden reached for the black pistol, but Maddie swept it away even as his fingertips grazed the handle.

She brought the gun around and clocked him on the side of the head. Braden saw black and swayed, his head sinking down into the grass. Everything was upside down. He blinked to clear his vision and prayed for strength. He knew he had to keep fighting, or she might kill him right now. That didn't seem like a Delta family move, but what did he really know about them besides the honorable way they'd treated him back in Colorado and his instincts that they were good people?

A door opened and he heard his next-door neighbor, Ensign Chaz who had a young wife and baby girl, call out, "Lieutenant Moyle? You okay?" About half of this neighborhood were Navy men or women and their families. Chaz wasn't in his line of command and that made it a lot easier to be friends and neighbors.

"Say you're okay or it's all over," Maddie whispered sweetly into his ear, pressing her body in close to his and the wrong end of the pistol into his neck.

Braden didn't know if she'd really shoot him, but she definitely had the upper hand, at the moment. "Doing good," Braden called back. "Just ... rolling around with my date."

"Oh?" A pause. "Oh, I see." Chaz chuckled. "Sorry for interrupting." The door closed quickly.

Maddie lifted the pistol away from him. "Your date looked pretty lame by the way. This is much more fun."

Braden would agree, if he would've been certain she wasn't going to shoot him.

"Now let's go inside and chat. Papa would say that I've had my fun and it's time to get to work."

She popped to her feet, shoved the gun in the holster, and offered him a hand up.

Braden had no idea if he dared take it.

"Come on," she urged. "I'm done play fighting for a minute."

Play fighting? What would she call real fighting? His hand

throbbed and was already swelling, he might have a broken rib, and his head was pounding from the hit with the gun. His pride had probably taken the worst hit as he'd been bested by a gorgeous woman he had six inches on and at least eighty pounds.

He took her hand, praying the respect and good feelings he'd had toward the Deltas in June weren't all delusional on his part.

She tugged and he climbed to his feet. She looked fresh and happy and untouched whereas he wanted some Ibuprofen and a few ice packs.

She smiled at him and released his hand, walking to his porch and picking up a girlie overnight bag and a floral purse, stepping onto the stoop and waiting for him to get the door. AS if every man would open her door and treat her like a lady. He hurried to open the door, feeling like he'd entered an alternate reality.

"Thank you, kind gentleman," she said, all sugar with just a hint of sass as she smiled up at him with those luscious lips.

Braden had the sudden insane urge to pin her against the door frame and see what those lips tasted like. He could bet a kiss or anytime spent with Maddie Delta would be nothing like his safe, nice, often boring, dinner dates.

She sauntered into the house, flipping on the light as she entered the open kitchen and living room, it was too small for a dining room but there was a four-person table in the kitchen and a sofa and loveseat in the living room. It was plenty of room for him. It seemed to shrink with this woman surveying his small home. Maddie Delta might look trim and was about five-six, but she was larger than life.

"Cute house," she said and it somehow wasn't demeaning at all for a tough, Navy sailor to be told his house was "cute". She looked into the open doorways of the two bedrooms with a shared bath between them and said, "This one on the right is mine? Looks like you're all settled in the bigger bedroom."

Wait ... what? Braden reared back and had no response as she strutted into the spare bedroom that his parents or sister had stayed in when they came to visit from Arizona this summer. She set her bag on the floor and her purse on the dresser and then walked back out.

"Now then." She spread her hands. "Where to start?" She looked him over. "Maybe I should take care of your injuries first. Papa told me not to hurt you, but I had to have a little fun." She shrugged.

If anyone was looking from the outside in she'd be the picture of innocent beauty. He was leery of that as his injuries attested she was not so innocent and had experience fighting he wished he could give to all of his men. Though some might be fooled by her beautiful face and sweet smile he could already tell she wasn't a woman he should underestimate. That assumption wasn't even based on her impressive fighting skills. He'd glimpsed it earlier but now it was even more obvious. There was something in her eyes that was ... disturbing.

She walked past him and into the kitchen. He edged closer to her, wanting answers more than anything. He also had to make sure she wasn't going to kill him.

Opening the freezer, she pulled out an ice pack and turned to him, holding it aloft. "What hurts the most? Your hand or your head?"

"Head," he admitted.

"Definitely need some ibuprofen then as well. Where do you

keep it?" She closed the freezer and opened a cupboard. "Glasses and bowls," she muttered, moving to the next cabinet door.

Braden moved quick. He wrapped his hands around her waist, spun her and pushed her against the fridge, trapping her hands at her sides and pressing his body against hers to hopefully stop her from lashing out. He kept his legs firmly together to prevent her from getting any ideas about kneeing him.

She blinked up at him and let the ice pack fall to the floor. "I like it," she said. "Quick and decisive, not ready to admit defeat, despite the humiliation of recently being beat up by a girl." She fluttered her eyelashes at him again. She was so good at mocking him but instead of burning with humiliation he was burning to stay close to her and kiss her long and slow. That wasn't smart on so many levels. "Maybe Papa's right and you will be an asset."

"I need some answers," he growled. An asset? He was busy and his Navy career was taking off. He wasn't taking a break to help the Delta family. He stared into her blue eyes and felt a tug he'd never felt in his life. He had the worrisome thought that this woman could get him to do anything she wanted.

"You don't need to prove anything to me though, I've seen your stats and your commendations and skills. Plus I already told you," she tantalizingly wet her lips with the tip of her tongue, "we'd get to know each other better and ... chat. I was just kindly trying to get you some ice and ibuprofen so you could be more comfortable and heal quicker."

"I don't trust you," he said softly, unable to stop his gaze from tracing over her face and studying the smooth skin, expressive blue eyes, thick eyelashes, and those lips that he was wanting a taste of more each moment. He blinked. He needed to clear his head and focus like he would at work or on a dangerous mission. This woman was very dangerous. He was unsure if she was a physical or emotional danger to him. Probably both.

"You're smart to be leery," she said, "It is a *crazy* world out there. But I promise you the Delta family are trustworthy and I, for one, have your back."

He studied her, unable to stop the laugh that gurgled out. "You just broke my hand, my rib, and gave me a concussion. Great teammate."

"Oh don't complain, handsome, you're better than that."

He shook his head and redirected. "Admiral Delta told me not to go after your family or your all-important secret. Why are you coming after me now?"

"We're concerned about Admiral Seamons."

He nodded. He was concerned for his inspiring leader as well. "That makes sense, with his wife being arrested and all the rumors about King Frederick." He should step back and release her, but it was much too exciting being close to this dangerous and alluring woman. She smelled like coconuts and sunshine. He should not let himself notice how she smelled or think of her as alluring. She was like Black Widow as a blonde.

"We'd appreciate any inside information you have and you keeping an eye out for us."

"A phone call wouldn't have sufficed?" He arched his eyebrows. Admiral Delta was concerned for his friend. Did he think Braden could protect him from the inside?

"I've been begging for this assignment for a couple months now."

"What assignment?" She'd said something about Jessie asking for the assignment earlier.

"Investigating Admiral Seamons and making ..." Her voice got low and husky. "Contact with you."

Investigate? So they weren't here to protect his CO but to join with those who speculated that if his wife was in cahoots with Frederick the admiral would be too. Braden would not support that but the way she said "contact" shot a thrill through him and overrode everything else for the moment.

Heat started in his chest and threatened to engulf him as Maddie arched up onto her tiptoes, her incredibly blue eyes focused on his. Any injuries were pushed to the back of his consciousness as he released his grip on her hands and cupped her face gently. Her face was soft under his palms and fingertips. After he devoured her incredible lips he wanted to take his time trailing kisses along her smooth cheeks and then down that tempting neck.

The scraping sound of the back door opening brought his head up.

Maddie's gaze sharpened, all traces of desire disappeared. "Expecting someone?" she whispered.

He shook his head.

Maddie edged around him, yanking the pistol from her hip. Braden turned to face whoever was coming and try to protect her. Though he wondered if any protection offered by him was superfluous to the training Maddie obviously had.

Two masked men rushed into the room, each holding guns. Braden's stomach clenched. What a night to not be carrying his pistol. He'd never make it to the bedroom to retrieve it in time to protect her.

"Drop it," the one man snarled.

Two rapid shots rang out as Braden tried to shelter Maddie with his body. The taller man slammed against the wall and released his gun, blood running down his shoulder. The other man's pistol flew in the air and blood sprayed the nearby window from the hit to his hand. Both guns clattered harmlessly to the floor.

"You first," Maddie said in the sweetest and most smart-alecky tone ever used by a beautiful, hilarious, and unsettling woman.

Braden's eyes widened as he realized neither of them had even gotten a shot off. He dashed across the room and swept the closest gun off the floor. The man with the hand wound scrambled away from him and darted through the laundry room. He banged out the back door.

Braden kicked the other gun away from the man on the floor.

"You got him?" Maddie called as she ran after the escapee with her gun in hand.

"Yes," was all Braden could manage before she was gone. He pointed the pistol at the man sitting against his wall and grasping his shoulder, glaring at Braden. This guy was hurting but not afraid. It was obvious he regretted that he'd lost the gun and failed his assignment.

Maddie cruised through the back door and was gone. Braden tried to catalogue what had just happened as he prayed she returned unharmed and with the other guy in tow. He wished he'd darted after the man escaping and left her here guarding this guy. She'd reacted so quickly he'd lost his chance. It grated at him. He was the leader, the decisive action man, not the sit and hold the gun on the man who was already incapacitated kind of guy.

Braden could only stew about everything Maddie had said as he waited. She claimed she'd come after him to get information about Admiral Seamons, but Braden knew his commanding officer. If Seamons wasn't loyal and good to the bone, America might as well wave the white flag to the world now. No way was his admiral a traitor and in league with King Frederick. No way.

There was also the humiliating fact that Maddie had bested Braden, shot both of these guys in the blink of an eye, and gone after the guy before Braden could make that move. Their roles right now were probably exactly what they should be. She was the Lieutenant and he was the new recruit following orders. He'd had to learn to follow orders to exactness in his military career but he definitely preferred giving the orders. Following Maddie's orders wouldn't be tough, especially if she'd let him cup her soft cheeks in his hands again, lean in, and kiss her.

The back door opened and he startled. His heart leapt and he was shocked how invested he was in her. Maddie Delta. He was far too taken with her and had wanted that kiss earlier as badly as he'd ever wanted anything. He tried to school his expression so she didn't know how gone he was in a matter of minutes. She'd probably only laugh at him. And he should be concerned that there was something off about her, something dark that he hadn't seen any of the other Deltas.

"Lieutenant?" It was Ensign Chaz. Such a good guy. "I heard shots." The man edged into the room. His eyes widened, taking in the injured man, Braden pointing a gun at him, and the blood all over the wall and floor. He backed away.

"We've got it under control," Braden said. "Go home and watch over your family."

"Okay." Chaz's gaze flitted to the masked and injured man on the floor and then back to Braden. "Should I call it in?"

"My girl is all over it," Braden told him confidently. He had no right to call Maddie his "girl" but he instinctively knew that she'd get ahold of Admiral Delta and whoever the Deltas sent to contain the situation would be more experienced than the local police. They'd know the right questions to ask and what to do with these two men.

Now if only "his girl" would get back here.

Find *Accepted* on Amazon.

Also by Cami Checketts

Delta Family Romances

Deceived

Abandoned

Committed

Betrayed

Devoted

Compromised

Endangered

Accepted

Returned

Devastated

Famous Friends Romances

Loving the Firefighter

Loving the Athlete

Loving the Rancher

Loving the Coach

Loving the Contractor

Loving the Sheriff

Loving the Entertainer

The Hidden Kingdom Romances

Royal Secrets

Only Her Undercover Spy

Only Her Cowboy

Only Her Best Friend

Only Her Blue-Collar Billionaire

Only Her Injured Stuntman

Only Her Amnesiac Fake Fiancé

Only Her Hockey Legend

Only Her Smokejumper Firefighter

Only Her Christmas Miracle

Jewel Family Romance

Do Marry Your Billionaire Boss

Do Trust Your Special Ops Bodyguard

Do Date Your Handsome Rival

Do Rely on Your Protector

Do Kiss the Superstar

Do Tease the Charming Billionaire

Do Claim the Tempting Athlete

Do Depend on Your Keeper

Strong Family Romance

Don't Date Your Brother's Best Friend

Her Loyal Protector

Don't Fall for a Fugitive

Her Hockey Superstar Fake Fiance

Don't Ditch a Detective

Don't Miss the Moment

Don't Love an Army Ranger

Don't Chase a Player

Don't Abandon the Superstar

Steele Family Romance

Her Dream Date Boss

The Stranded Patriot

The Committed Warrior

Extreme Devotion

Quinn Family Romance

The Devoted Groom

The Conflicted Warrior

The Gentle Patriot

The Tough Warrior

Her Too-Perfect Boss

Her Forbidden Bodyguard

Running Romcom

Running for Love

Taken from Love

Saved by Love

Cami's Collections

Hidden Kingdom Romance Collection

Survive the Romance Collection

Mystical Lake Resort Romance Collection

Counterfeit Date

Snow Valley

Full Court Devotion: Christmas in Snow Valley

A Touch of Love: Summer in Snow Valley

Running from the Cowboy: Spring in Snow Valley

Light in Your Eyes: Winter in Snow Valley

Romancing the Singer: Return to Snow Valley

Fighting for Love: Return to Snow Valley

Other Books by Cami

Seeking Mr. Debonair: Jane Austen Pact

Seeking Mr. Dependable: Jane Austen Pact

Saving Sycamore Bay

Oh, Come On, Be Faithful

Protect This

Blog This

Redeem This

The Broken Path

Dead Running

Dying to Run

Fourth of July

Love & Loss

Love & Lies

About the Author

Cami is a part-time author, part-time exercise consultant, part-time housekeeper, full-time wife, and overtime mother of four adorable boys. Sleep and relaxation are fond memories. She's never been happier.

Join Cami's VIP list to find out about special deals, giveaways and new releases and receive a free copy of *Rescued by Love: Park City Firefighter Romance* by clicking here.

cami@camichecketts.com

www.camichecketts.com

Made in United States
Orlando, FL
30 March 2023

31546536R00113